ALSO BY
RANDA ABDEL-FATTAH

WHERE THE STREETS HAD A NAME

RANDA ABDEL-FATTAH

SCHOLASTIC PRESS
NEW YORK

First published in Australia by Pan Macmillan Australia Pty Ltd in 2008.
Published by arrangement with Marion Lloyd Books, an imprint of Scholastic,
a division of Scholastic Ltd. Published in the UK in 2009.

Library of Congress Cataloging-in-Publication Data

Abdel-Fattah, Randa.
Where the streets had a name / by Randa Abdel-Fattah. — 1st ed.
    p.   cm.
Summary: Thirteen-year-old Hayaat of Bethlehem faces checkpoints,
curfews, and the travel permit system designed to keep people on the
West Bank when she attempts to go to her grandmother's ancestral home
in Jerusalem with her best friend.
    ISBN 978-0-545-17292-9
    [1. Family life — Bethlehem — Fiction.   2. Palestinian Arabs — Fiction.
3. Arab-Israeli conflict — 1993 — Fiction.   4. West Bank — Fiction.]   I. Title.
    PZ7.A15892Whe   2010
    [Fic] — dc22

                                                                          2009043122

            10 9 8 7 6 5 4 3 2 1   10 11 12 13 14

                    Printed in the U.S.A.   23
                Reinforced Binding for Library Use
                    First edition, November 2010
                    Book design by Lillie Howard

To my grandmother Sitti Jamilah,
who passed away on April 24, 2008, aged 98.
I had hoped you could live to see this book
and that you would be allowed to touch
the soil of your homeland again.
It is my consolation that you died
surrounded by my father and family
and friends who cherished you.
May you rest in peace.

And to my father —
may you see a free Palestine
in your lifetime.

ONE

It's six-thirty in the morning. I stumble out of bed and splash cold water on my flushed face. The portable fan has been switched off during the night, probably by Sitti Zeynab, who sleeps with a thick blanket even in the sweltering summer nights. I grab my sister's toothbrush. For the past weeks we have been sharing, and Mama was disorganized during last night's lifting of the curfew, so I still don't have a new one.

We were permitted to leave our houses for two hours. We raced to Abu Yusuf's grocery store. By Baba's calculations we had one hour and fifteen minutes to stock up, load the shopping into our car, and return home. Sitti Zeynab wanted to come. But it takes her an entire broadcast of Al-Jazeerah to raise her eighty-six-year-old body from her armchair and walk to the toilet. Two hours don't cater to the Sitti Zeynabs of this world.

With three-month-old Mohammed nestled close to her chest in a makeshift sling, Mama delegated. She sent me to the bread section. Baba, holding the hand of my seven-year-old brother, Tariq, was sent to toiletries. Jihan, my older sister, was sent to household cleaning products.

Mama dealt with the rest.

Baba bought five tubes of 2-in-1 shampoo, a dozen bars of soap, disposable razors, sanitary pads, diapers, toothpaste, and toilet paper. In his panicked rush (Tariq wanted to play), he forgot a new toothbrush for me. I didn't complain. After all, the diapers were one size too small. Mohammed had it worse.

Abu Yusuf stood behind the cash register with his wife and son, trying to cope with the mass of people falling over the counter with their goods, pushing and shoving to be served first. Jihan and I giggled at Abu Yusuf, whose face was flushed bright red as he jabbed at the keys of the cash register while yelling out orders to his son and answering people's questions about where to find lemon-scented detergent and three-ply toilet paper. Two women started yelling at each other, claiming first right to be served.

"Order!" Um Yusuf cried out wearily. "When will we ever learn to stand in line?"

Baba rolled his eyes at me.

Mama approached us, her arms overflowing with goods. "Why aren't you at the cash register?" she shrieked. "We don't have much time left!"

Baba shrugged and Mama looked as though she might clobber him with the jar of pickles she held.

"Look at them," he said, gesturing at the mob of shoppers. "We will be trampled and I'm wearing my best suit. I picked it out especially. You never know who you will meet when a curfew is lifted."

Mama snorted. "Trampled? Better to be flattened here than be out on the streets when the curfew is back on."

Jihan's eyes met mine. I could tell that she found it as difficult as I to believe that anybody could flatten Mama. Sure enough, Mama pushed and heaved her body through until she reached the counter.

As I brush my teeth with Jihan's worn, bristly toothbrush, I look in the mirror. It always seems as though a stranger is looking back at me. I stare at the twisted, contorted skin around my right cheek, the scarring that zigzags across my forehead. I raise a hand and cover the right side of my face. The left is mostly smooth. Normal. Slowly, I lower my hand and I am a stranger to myself again.

I spit the toothpaste into the basin. Then I gargle three times, clean my nose, wash my face, pass water over the crown of my head, rub water on my arms, up to my elbows. Over the scab with the texture of tree bark that decorates my right elbow. A scab earned when I fell from a windowsill. Samy had thought I'd be too afraid to sneak into the teacher's lounge and pinch some sweets from the platter the teachers had left on the table. I wasn't scared — but when I tumbled off the sill on my way out, I did drop the baklava. Samy still ate it, though. He just dusted off the dirt.

My long, thick braid dances from side to side down my back. I look down at my socks, sticking out from under the red nightgown that used to be Jihan's. I'm too lazy to wash my feet, the last action required to complete the ablution before prayer.

God is forgiving of children, I say to myself.

Sitti Zeynab is not so forgiving. But then again, she need never know.

Sitti Zeynab farts. A lot.

She shares a room with Jihan, Tariq, and me. My sister, brother, and I share a double bed. I wet the bed the other night, after another nightmare. Jihan was, understandably, furious. She helped me change the sheets, though, and swore under her breath, rather than at me. The next morning she argued with my parents that she wanted her own bed. But according to Mama and Baba, a new bed is "not a priority." (When the Israelis confiscated our land in Beit Sahour, we moved to a small house in a poor neighborhood in Bethlehem. Our house now has two bedrooms instead of four and we're living off Baba and Mama's savings.) Baba walked away from the argument with Jihan, and Mama warned her to hold her tongue. "Baba does not need to hear you whine," she scolded. In Jihan's defense, I pointed out to Mama that she had only the night before complained to Baba that the hallway carpet needed replacing. She sent me to the bedroom with a basket of washing to fold. I'm sent to my room quite regularly.

Sitti Zeynab sleeps on the single bed. It has a pine headboard decorated with glossy magazine stickers of Amr Diab, Nancy Ajram, Leonardo DiCaprio, and Michael Jackson. Sitti Zeynab complains that the pouted lips, plastic bodies, and gyrating hips will repel the angels. She once woke up with a yelp, having opened her eyes to find Diab's permanently frozen, twinkling eyes and dimpled grin staring down at her.

Sitti Zeynab goes to bed at ten o'clock every night. After she has performed the last prayer and read some pages of the Koran, she heaves her large body up onto the bed. It's difficult for her to raise her legs. Of course, that's because she's old and inflexible, but Jihan and I think it's also because her boobs are so heavy that they get in the way. When Sitti Zeynab finally manages to lie down, her head sinks into the pillow and she bellows, *"Ya Rab!"* Her chest wheezes with the effort of movement; a fart is often a welcome relief for her.

They are almost always loud. Not necessarily smelly. Jihan and I have perfected our defenses. Heads under the blanket; laughs stifled. The occasional spray of cheap air freshener over our pillows. Tariq never holds back, though. "I will ask the Israelis for a gas mask, Sitti Zeynab!"

Sitti Zeynab is sitting on the edge of the bed as I walk back into the bedroom to put on my school uniform. Jihan is still asleep, the blanket drawn over her face, a few strands of her hair spilling over the top. The corner of a picture of her fiancé, Ahmad, protrudes from under her pillow. Jihan's feet are squashed in Tariq's face. His mouth is wide open, his hands tucked close to his chest.

Sitti Zeynab smiles at me and says: "Your hair is long and beautiful, *Masha Allah*. God be praised. You have hair other girls can only dream about."

"Too thick. I want fair hair."

"Ahh, but the one-eyed is always a beauty in the land of the blind."

I shrug. "I need a toothbrush."

"And I need a hip replacement. That is life." She stares back at me, lifts herself an inch off the bed, and farts.

"*Yaa!* That *mansaf*. Oof! It always makes me windy."

*   *   *

I help my grandmother to the living room. She carefully edges her behind onto a chair.

"Oh God!" she cries. "Ease these bones of mine."

"Do you want some breakfast, Sitti Zeynab?"

She pats her stomach with both hands. "Too early," she says, her face scrunching up at the thought. "Maybe later . . . yes, maybe later . . . Oh! But you eat!" She is suddenly agitated. "Strength, my darling, you must eat. You're so thin."

"Yes, Sitti Zeynab," I mutter.

"You must fill your stomach before school. Otherwise your brains will stay asleep. You need to wake them out of bed with some cheese and bread! How else will you become a doctor? Or was it a university lecturer? I can never remember. . . ."

As my ambitions don't extend to either profession, I refrain from responding.

"Why are you still standing there? *Yallah!* Go eat!"

I hurry into the kitchen and hear her praise God as the refrigerator door creaks open. I make myself a cup of sweet mint tea and eat a slice of feta cheese and some pitted black olives wedged in a chunky piece of bread.

While I'm eating, Mama comes in and kisses me on the forehead. She's a heavy woman and also a chain-smoker. When she's not eating, she's smoking. Sometimes she does both simultaneously. Mama is always breathless. She shares her mother's misfortune and has a chest like a tank. It presses up against her so that the words struggle to escape from her mouth. But this morning she speaks as though time is chasing after her and she cannot waste a single word.

"Good morning, *ya* Hayaat. Did you sleep well? Make Sitti Zeynab a cup of tea. Mohammed's poo is a funny color today. Did you hear him crying last night? Oh, school is closed; there is a curfew. We will need to rearrange our supplies. Go easy on the toilet paper. Your father didn't buy enough. Thank God I have my cigarettes. Wipe the crumbs off the bench."

I think about the pros and cons of the curfew. On the one hand, there's the boredom. Always the boredom of being stuck at home. Home means chores and dealing with Mama and Baba's boredom. "Clean your room. Help me rearrange the kitchen cabinets. Do your homework. Go inside and study. Stop fighting with Jihan and Tariq. Would you peel the potatoes please, *ya Hayaat?* No? Did you say no? Peel them now!"

Then there's the important matter of meeting my friend Samy's latest dare to stick a potato in the exhaust pipe of Ostaz Hany's car. Not one of the peeled potatoes. Any potato will do.

Maybe this seems cruel, but Ostaz Hany picks his nose and teaches us mathematics, so it's not such a bad thing to have a potato in the exhaust pipe of his car.

On the other hand, I'll have a break from school, and this is also not such a bad thing. "I won't see Khader for a while, then," I whisper to myself.

"Who is Khader?" Mama asks.

Tariq runs in and grins up at me. "Khader is a pig. He is the poo of a pig. He is the insect that feeds on the poo of a pig."

I smile at him. His moral support is endearing.

"Don't use such language, boy!" Mama yells.

"But he calls her potato mash face! He is *khara*."

Mama hits Tariq on the nape of his neck. "Enough! Where did you come up with such filthy language?"

"Yesterday you told Khalto Samar that the bathroom smells like *khara* because —"

"Enough!" Mama fixes him with her death stare and he walks out, a puzzled look on his face.

"Oh God!" Sitti Zeynab cries from the living room. "How can Hayaat learn when there is so much disruption?" For such an old woman I marvel at her hearing sometimes.

"*Yaama*, don't make it worse." Mama rolls her eyes and lights a cigarette. She slumps down onto a chair, stretches out her legs, and inhales, closing her eyes and throwing her head back. "These wretched curfews," she mutters to the ceiling. "Being trapped with family for longer than is humanly possible. I will be stuck with your whining father; my annoying mother; a crying baby; an energetic son; and a lovesick, dieting daughter. God only knows how long they will decide to keep it going this time."

"Baba is not a whiner, *Yaama*."

Mama looks closely at me. "Do you know what he did this morning, Hayaat? I was simply trying to explain to him that there is an efficient way to extract toothpaste from a tube and he sighed and walked away!"

'I am not having a conversation about toothpaste,' he muttered! Ah! But he didn't understand that it was a conversation about toothpaste being squirted out of a tube and splashed down onto a basin I will inevitably have to clean!"

I switch off. I'm used to Mama's rambling complaints about my father. When Mama's tirade has finished, she turns to me and says: "*Habibti*, you are my precious one. May God find you a good boy one day who will ignore your scars and love you for who you are on the inside."

Mama sucks on her cigarette and smiles affectionately at me, then walks into the living room to join Sitti Zeynab.

I make Sitti Zeynab a cup of tea and take it to her.

"God reward you and heal your face," she says.

I grit my teeth and plonk myself down into a chair. Although the curfew is only hours old, I'm already bored — and if I hear one more reference to my face, I'll scream.

Jihan soon wakes and stumbles into the living room, rubbing the sleep out of her eyes.

"Mama, Ahmad called last night. He has found a reception hall in Ramallah. But he wants me to approve it first. Can I go?"

"Baba and I will come too."

"Mama!"

"Do you think you'll go alone?" Mama snaps. "Just because you have *katb al-kitaab* doesn't mean you're married in the eyes of the community! That day has not yet come. Huh! And what if they block the roads and you're stuck in Ramallah? Or what if you're delayed at Qalandiya checkpoint or not allowed through? Think, *ya* Jihan, before you speak and maybe I won't need to smoke so many cigarettes!"

"It's not fair!" Jihan screeches, dramatically sinking into a chair. "From the moment he proposed it's been like this. Citizenship application? *Rejected.* Where to live? Where to work? Which road to take? Blue pass–road or West Bank pass–road? I will grow a head of gray hair by the time I'm married."

The problem is that Ahmad is an Israeli Arab from Lod. He lives and works there. But Jihan, a West Banker, can't obtain Israeli citizenship. So they've decided that as Lod is closer to Ramallah than to Bethlehem, they'll live in Ramallah so that Ahmad can keep his job. The wedding will also be in Ramallah, as it's impossible for Jihan to obtain the permit to enter Lod even if it's only for her wedding.

Before Ahmad arrived on the scene, Mama and Baba brought several Bethlehem suitors to Jihan, but she rolled her eyes at each one. This one's mustache was too thick. That one's jawline was too weak. Each suitor had a problem: "Only speaks of politics." So Mama and Baba brought one who didn't. "Only speaks of bodybuilding." The complaints went on: "This one doesn't know who Amr Diab is!" "That one thinks Sitti Zeynab is charming!"

Mama and Baba gave up. Then Jihan bumped into Ahmad — literally. Having come to Bethlehem to attend a wedding of a mutual friend, Ahmad accidentally tripped over her on the dance floor. Three hours later Jihan declared to my parents that she had fallen in love. Mama and Baba spent the next days frantically attending to the necessary investigations: Who was his family? Were they decent, reputable people? Did he work? Could he provide for their precious daughter?

Hany Abdullah, the civil engineer, could vouch for the excellent reputation of Ahmad's family. Amir, the restaurant owner, could attest to Ahmad's manners and scandal-free past, so the *al-Fatiha* was read a month later and Jihan has spent every night since admiring the way her ring sparkles under the lightbulb above the kitchen stove.

"Well, will you come with me today to find a new outfit?" Jihan says. "I hate all my clothes. Every single one!"

"Our feet can't even touch the street," Mama tells Jihan dryly. "So forget leaving the house today." Mama turns to Sitti Zeynab and says: "Why did she have to fall in love with a man from the outside?"

Sitti Zeynab gives Mama a sober look and nods agreement. "A Bethlehem boy would have been so much easier."

"I can't choose who I love!"

"You could have chosen Soliman!" Sitti Zeynab says. "What was wrong with him? Did you not notice his eyes were like melted chocolate? And he was polite and tall, which a man must be if possible, and most wonderful of all was that he had a job."

"Why didn't you marry him yourself if he was so perfect?" Jihan snaps.

Sitti Zeynab grins. She's become accustomed to Jihan's fiery temper. "He wouldn't be able to keep up with me, *ya habibti*."

Jihan tries to suppress a giggle.

Mama sighs. "Yes, but, *habibti*, it would have been so much easier if you had fallen in love with somebody from here. You will move to Ramallah. And I will kiss you on your wedding night and never see you again."

"Oh, Mama, stop being so dramatic. You can always visit me."

"Yes, spend hours on the road and battle Qalandiya checkpoint with Mohammed. Qalandiya? By the time I arrive, my nerves will be frazzled, I will enter your home in a bad mood, and Ahmad will complain to his mother about his ill-tempered mother-in-law. And then you will be upset with him for talking badly about me. An argument will ensue, as I know you will leap to my defense, and your domestic bliss will be ruined. So, you see, my darling, this whole Ramallah business is just a disaster."

Jihan covers her face with her hands and groans.

Sitti Zeynab leans forward. "Tell her about the pickled cucumbers."

"Eh?"

"The pickled cucumbers!" Sitti Zeynab says breathlessly, sinking back into her chair.

"Ohh! Yes. Not to mention the problem of how I am to make you my jars of pickled cucumbers! You know how much Ahmad loves them. He told me that he preferred them over his mother's. Hers are too salty, he says. Did you know he said that?"

"No, he never mentioned it," Jihan says in a bored tone.

"Well, he did. So I can't even pamper my son-in-law with my excellent pickles."

"Simply buy a box of cucumbers and by the time you get through the checkpoints from here to Ramallah, they will have pickled on their own." Jihan winks at me.

"Hmm, yes, maybe," Sitti Zeynab says seriously. "But they will probably ruin in a cardboard box."

Jihan rolls her eyes and then suddenly lets out a wail. "I miss him! I want to see him!"

"Your fiancé must wait," Mama says.

"Waiting will make him desire you more," Sitti Zeynab says solemnly.

"Desire isn't what is missing in our relationship. We have too much desire! It is suffocating!" She throws her hands up in frustration. "I want to be able to see him whenever I feel like it. To drink coffee with him in a café and have people walk by and envy the way he caresses my hand."

Mama and Sitti Zeynab let out hoots of laughter. Jihan scowls at them. "What's so funny? My tormented existence is not funny!"

"Your *tormented* existence," Mama repeats, letting out another shriek of laughter. "Oh, what a luxury it is to be young and so indulgent with words!"

"What would you know about torment, *ya* Jihan?" Sitti Zeynab says. "Such unbridled self-pity!"

Jihan stands and turns on her heel, and I scurry after her.

"I would rather the Zionists than that old hag!" she whispers in my ear.

TWO

Baba sits in his armchair, his eyes fixed on a piece of paper in his hand. I'm not close enough to see the writing, but I don't have to. I know he's holding the title deeds to our land. He strokes the edges like a child stroking a kitten.

I want to throw myself onto his lap and beg him to tell me a story. A story that starts with "Once upon a time." A story he heard his grandfather tell as the men sat winters and winters ago in the front courtyard of their stone house, exhaling rings of *argeela* smoke like drowsy dragons, swapping folktales, singing the song of the *oud*, and telling one another about the beat of the *daraboka*.

When I was little, I climbed the olive trees on the twenty *dunams* of land my father owned in Beit Sahour, a town not far from Bethlehem. Tariq was in Mama's womb then, and I'm sure he jealously sucked his fingers as he heard me swinging from one branch to the next as I ignored Mama's pleas to climb down and play with dolls or read a book. My grandfather Abu Hasan had scolded Baba for the same thing many summers ago. And his father, Abu Murad, had pressed the olives and tended the soil many autumns before that. The land was green and fertile, and more than one hundred olive trees stretched their roots down into the soil.

"They are holy trees," Baba used to say. "Part of our heritage. They are also mentioned in the Koran. Mary, beloved mother of Jesus, peace be upon him, took refuge under an olive tree when the pangs of her labor were too much to bear."

"It was a palm tree, Baba," I corrected.

"Are you sure?"

"Yes, I learned this in school. She shook the leaves of the palm tree in Bethlehem and ate the dates."

"Oh . . . Well, palm trees or olive trees, what's the difference? The roots of this land are holy. Oh, and, Hayaat?"

"Mmm?"

"Don't mention this to your teacher."

After the harvest, I would watch in amazement as the olives were ground into paste beneath two huge rolling stones. Then Baba and his workers would spread the pulp on circular straw mats and load the mats into a press that squeezed the paste to produce thick, yellow-green, fragrant oil, which was later collected in big plastic containers. Mama would invite our friends to breakfast to eat *zaatar*, bread, cheese, and hummus. Baba would sit at the head of the table, watching our guests eat, imploring them to dip the bread in oil, to eat more. His face would beam as the corners of the guests' mouths glistened with the delicious oil.

One day I begged Baba to take me with him in the morning. We drove out to our land while the sun was still sleeping. Baba told me to stop babbling. "Roll down your window and just listen," he said. "But it's quiet," I said, confused. "Yes. Listen to the quiet."

I listened to the quiet and looked out at Jebel Abu Ghneim, a mountain encircled by softly rolling hills and valleys. Baba told me that before the vegetation was torn down to make way for a settlement it was a thickly forested, luscious green mountain.

"Who lived there, Baba?" I asked. I liked to imagine it had been full of fairies and tree creatures who had parties during the night and sprinkled magic on the trees.

"There are many Christian holy sites on the mountain," Baba explained. "Shepherd's Fields, Saint Theodore's Well, the Byzantine monastery, and the Church of Bir Qadisum, where Mary dismounted before giving birth to Jesus. Tell that to your teacher!"

I found this information too dull, preferring instead to imagine my flying fairies.

"Did you know that the sun asks God for permission to rise and set every day, *ya* Hayaat?" Baba asked me as we sat under an olive tree, watching the horizon burst over Jebel Abu Ghneim in an explosion of red, orange, and coral. It warmed me to sit beside Baba and watch God's permission unfold.

Baba told me the forest had been torn down before I was born. I imagined my fairies and tree creatures waking to the crushing weight of a Caterpillar D9 bulldozer, preparing the way for new settlements and exclusive bypass roads.

My memory of Beit Sahour is like a patchwork quilt

filled with holes. But my memories of Mama there are the brightest and most colorful. I once rose early from bed to find her in her sewing room, bent over layers of material stretched over her lap, her face scrunched up in concentration. She was wearing the same clothes as the day before; her hair, dyed henna red, flowed loosely down her back, her bangs swept back by the glasses perched on her head. I asked her if she had slept that night and she smiled, stretching her arms up to the ceiling, a mischievous twinkle in her eye. "I was bored with the curtains in my bedroom. So I have spent the last twelve hours making new ones." She never stopped. She made new upholstery for the living room, quilts for our beds, shawls for Sitti Zeynab to wear in winter, baby blankets for friends. She rose early with Baba and cooked hot breakfasts of fried beans, eggs, minced meat encircled by creamy hummus, and warm bread drizzled with olive oil and thyme. Baba and Mama would eat, and when they were finished Baba would leave for the field. When Jihan, Tariq, Sitti Zeynab, and I woke two hours later, another breakfast would be spread on the table and Sitti Zeynab would sit with us, her hawklike gaze daring us not to eat.

In Beit Sahour, Mama was filled with a restless energy. She sewed, she potted in her garden beds. She cooked as though each day was Ramadan.

When that old life was gone, crushed under the new settler road, I wondered if Mama would change. We moved to Bethlehem where Baba hoped he might find work, and Mama cried and cursed and then, one day, stopped. I think she realized that we would never return to Beit Sahour and that she was better off putting her energy into bossing us around and running the house as though a reproachful mother-in-law were watching over her.

Baba, on the other hand, did change. He mourned the loss of his olive grove like a parent mourning a child. In Beit Sahour, he was loud and jocular. Working on his land made him happy and we felt that happiness when he came home to us in the evening. But in our apartment in Bethlehem, Baba sits in silence, sucking on his *argeela* or flicking through the news channels.

When we lost our land, he imploded.

We have no way of seeing the evidence of his demolition — the rubble and ruins are inside him — but he no longer talks and laughs and tells stories as he did before.

He continues to wake early, a habit from the days he tended to his farm before sunrise. He eats breakfast with us, but his movements are those of a self-conscious guest, because he has never known our house in the early hours of the morning. And so after breakfast he usually leaves, returning in the late afternoon for the main meal, *ghada.* He eats quickly and quietly. After that he collects a few pieces of coal from a bag in the laundry room and places them on the stove. Low heat, delicately balanced. He empties the head of the *argeela* and stuffs it with fresh apple tobacco. He squashes the tobacco in and then covers it with a small piece of foil. Tariq or I are assigned the task of finding him a toothpick. He then pricks the foil with several openings. Next, he refills the glass with fresh water. "Can't you do that somewhere else?" Mama scolds. "I'm trying to wash the dishes." But every night he repeats the procedure in the kitchen and every night she scolds.

When the coal is gray and alive with heat, he picks it up with his tongs and places it on the foil, pressing down. Our apartment building has a front porch on the first floor that overlooks a small communal garden. Baba carries the *argeela* to the porch and sits on the green bench, legs extended before him, one foot curled over the other.

Mama sent me to follow him once after breakfast. "Go alone," she said. "For it will bring shame to this family if anyone knew I sent you."

I told Samy anyway.

We followed Baba to Frères Street, the highest point in Bethlehem. Baba walked slowly but purposefully, his hands thrust deep into the pockets of his gray trousers. He led us to Bethlehem University, to a high point fenced by railings. I drew a sharp breath as I saw the landscape before me: a panoramic view of Jebel Abu Ghneim covered with settlements.

Baba leaned his elbow on the railings and looked at the horizon in silence, like a man standing at a headstone in a cemetery.

He stood there for half an hour, unnaturally still and barely moving.

Samy knew enough to remain silent.

On his way home, Baba stopped at a coffee shop. He

took his cell phone out of his shirt pocket and called a friend. Abu Hussein arrived shortly afterward. Samy and I watched them order mint tea and an *argeela* each.

When Mama asked me where Baba went, I told her about the coffee shop only.

The curfew lasts for several more days. My parents fight over everything. Mohammed's diaper rash. Jihan's wedding plans. Failing to stock up on enough feta cheese and bread. Putting too much sugar in the tea. Putting too little.

Jihan does her exercises in the cramped living room. Sit-ups, jumping jacks, and jogging in place. She lifts cans of chickpeas and jugs of laundry detergent for muscle toning. When she can get away with it, she replaces meals with cigarettes (sucked up secretly behind the water tank on the rooftop of our house). She has to stay hidden from the soldiers and from my parents, who strongly disapprove of smoking unless they are the ones doing it. Jihan is determined to lose weight before her wedding and is prepared to take on the Israel Defense Forces to do so. She should be more frightened of Mama and Baba.

Sitti Zeynab sits in her armchair for days. She thinks Jihan has gone mad. "A little meat on a woman is nice. Do you want people to look at you on your wedding day and think you had a holiday in Gaza?"

Jihan grits her teeth and presses on with her jumping jacks.

"But I am just an old woman," Sitti Zeynab says, grinning at Baba, who's too absorbed in his *argeela* to interfere. "Why would the freshly hatched Jihan bother to listen to the wrinkled?"

"First intelligent thing she's said in months," Jihan mutters to me.

During the curfew, Sitti Zeynab only leaves her chair to pray, go to the toilet, and go to bed. She has an opinion about everything. Each day Mama finishes a pack of cigarettes before the sun sets and tries her best not to kill Sitti Zeynab or Baba.

I spend the curfew nights in front of the television, doing my homework. We're studying world music in English. My teacher is a Michael Jackson fan and loves the song "Remember the Time." Our homework is to write our own song based on times we remember. I remember the time I was voted the best dancer in my class. I dance the *dabka*, a traditional folk dance, and when I dance I feel as though my feet have little wings on them. Light but controlled, I know my routines by heart. One step forward, bend at the knee, kick with the right foot, one step again.

I also remember when Mohammed was born and Mama bit Baba's arm during a contraction and drew blood. Baba was not allowed to so much as grimace.

I remember the time I saw my first — well, my first and only — movie at a theater. It was in Ramallah and it was not so hard to travel there then. The movie was called *The Princess Diaries*, and I ate all my popcorn and drank my can of Pepsi within the first fifteen minutes.

I remember Maysaa with her upside-down braid and buckteeth. I remember us in the playground showing the other girls some new *dabka* moves we'd learned in class. We formed a line and danced in a large circle around the playground, attracting new dancers as we sang:

O, you who passed by and waved with the hand
You marked the secrets of love in my heart
I heard your voice when you talked
Like a bird singing on top of an olive tree.

Maysaa's tongue always protruded slightly from her mouth as she concentrated on her dance moves. I remember Maysaa, but that memory makes me sick because I also remember the day everything changed.

From that day, I've been the one who occasionally wets the bed. I'm the one who is subjected to a tsk-tsk, a depressed sigh, and an open prayer every time my aunts, uncles, and family friends gaze at my face. The women cup my chin in their hands, manufacture moistened eyes, and exhale loudly, killing me with their garlic or cigarette breath. "Your beauty snatched away. Wasted. Oh, my darling."

On the last night of the curfew, I wake with a start from a familiar nightmare. Jihan and Tariq are snoring gently beside me. I frantically lower my hand to the mattress. Thank God it's dry this time.

Maysaa's face had filled my dreams. She's like a faulty tap that won't stop dripping. You don't notice it until the stillness of the night.

I rub the beads of sweat from my face. Sitti Zeynab is farting and snoring in blissful ignorance of my pain.

It's about three in the morning and I need fresh air. This is understandable given that I sleep in a room filled with enough gas to light a stove.

I tiptoe out of my room, past my parents' bedroom. Mohammed is fast asleep in between Mama and Baba. I slowly open the front door and peek out.

A jeep is on patrol. I quickly shut the door and wait for it to pass. I wait. And wait. And when I'm sure that it's passed I wait a little longer. Finally, I open the door a fraction again. Three soldiers are now roaming the narrow street on foot. They're strapped with machine guns. They suddenly stop. Two of them look younger than Jihan; the third as old as my father. They huddle together and one of them passes the other two a cigarette. They light up and lean back against a broken stone fence in front of the dilapidated apartment buildings directly across from my home.

There's a deathly ghost-town kind of silence to the night. There are no cars or footsteps. No bats or owls or rustling of leaves. Perhaps bats and owls have curfew restrictions too. The soldiers' voices crash against the silent night.

One of the soldiers starts to tell a story. I can't help but stare and watch the transformation from soldier to human. His face lights up, vibrant and excitable. His gun jiggles up and down as he becomes more animated. The others roar with laughter.

I'm entranced. I lean my face against the door frame and stare at the trio, standing a mere twenty feet from me. For days I've only seen the faces of my family. I study the soldiers' faces: the shape of their noses, the color of their eyes, the contours of their cheekbones, and the stubble mapped around their chins. My eyes glaze over and I'm weightless, unaware of my physical self.

One of the soldiers sees me and, startled, points his gun at me. "Back, get inside!" he shouts in broken Arabic.

The other soldiers grab their guns and frantically look around, their eyes widening in panic. The stench of fear is in the air. My fear, their fear, in dangerous competition.

I anxiously step back inside the house, slamming the door behind me.

THREE

The curfew is finally lifted. School is open again.

Samy knocks loudly on the front door. *"Yallah, Hayaat!"* he hollers. "Come on."

I bound through the house and pass Mama, who, with a large loaf of bread under one arm and a screaming Mohammed in the other, yells at me to not run through the apartment.

"Make sure you drink up that knowledge," Sitti Zeynab cries.

"She only has education going for her now," I overhear Mama say to Sitti Zeynab with a heavy sigh. "For who will marry her with those scars?"

"Don't worry. Every pea has a pod," Sitti Zeynab says. "My Hayaat is royalty, I tell you."

"She could marry somebody blind," Tariq says innocently.

"Don't be *abeet*," Jihan scolds. *Abeet*, dumb, is her standard label for Tariq. "We have standards too!"

I rush out of the apartment building and almost knock Samy off his feet. The first to accept a dare, lose his temper, and bring a teacher to tears of exasperation, Samy is skinny and pale, his face framed by a heavy mane of wild black curls. His eyebrows are thick and black and hang over his small gray eyes. They say that his eyes were filled with color before the imprisonment of his father when he was six and the death of his mother from a heart attack soon after. We moved to Bethlehem when I was nine and so I never knew Samy's parents.

They say that Samy's father was the type of person who commanded respect. "When he spoke, he inspired even the most foolish empty-head," Um Ziyad, owner of the local bread store, informed my parents when we moved in and Mama and Baba were offered an exposition on the scandals of the surrounding homes. "Even the most lazy twit, my son included," she told them, "was inspired to go on strike after reading one of Abu Samy's essays or hearing him at a public address."

They say Samy saw his father being dragged out of the house by agents from the Israeli internal security service, the *Shabak*. Somebody informed on him. That was common enough. The *Shabak* agents came in the evening. They beat Samy's father and then took him away. Samy never speaks about it. Maybe he's too young to remember the details. I have never dared ask.

Samy lives with his uncle and aunt, Amo Joseph and Amto Christina. They're childless. They do charity work at their church on Saturdays and Sundays, run religious workshops on weekdays, coordinate the replanting of uprooted olive trees in their spare time, and volunteer at the United Nations Relief and Works Agency after dinner. According to Mama they're also "creating the cure for cancer, sewing up the ozone hole, and bringing democracy to the Middle East."

Amo Joseph and Amto Christina are both short and thin, and look more like brother and sister than husband and wife. They believe that television is the work of the devil and music is the devil's hobby. Hymns and nationalistic songs are approved. Cartoons, Hollywood movies, and Arabic *X Factor* are not. Consequently,

Samy and I have spent a lot of time trying to formulate a convincing argument to persuade Amo Joseph and Amto Christina that watching television will not result in us stewing over burning coals.

Baba likes Amo Joseph because when Amo Joseph's not saving Palestine, he's smoking his *argeela*. They never discuss religion. They sometimes discuss politics. They always discuss the "good old days," and most conversations include some mention of olive trees and figs.

Mama likes Amto Christina and Amo Joseph but disapproves of my friendship with Samy because he's "always scowling" and can regularly be heard arguing with Amto Christina and Amo Joseph about anything from leaving wet towels on the bathroom floor to going to church without brushing his hair.

Maybe Jewish mothers also disapprove of their daughters spending their spare time with boys, I don't know, but there are many times I've overheard Mama complain to Baba that it's unnatural for me to be so friendly with a boy. "She is still too young to know of such things," Baba tells her.

"Yes," she replies, "but it is better to stop it now,

before they both become aware. She has no girlfriends, *ya* Foad. Not since . . . Well, she hates to be around girls. She hates to be around anybody except Samy! It is wrong, *ya* Foad."

"Nur! Think for a moment. Is it not obvious why she does not like to be around girls?"

"Well, yes, but there is something wrong about their friendship. It is too strong. I don't like it. . . . It frightens me."

"Pah! They are both children, so let them enjoy their innocence while they still have it."

For now Baba's view prevails and Mama is left to sigh melodramatically every time I tell her I'm outside playing with Samy.

This morning Samy is not interested in how I spent my time during the curfew. All he wants to know is which contestant has been eliminated on *X Factor*.

"I'll race you to school," I cry, after I've painstakingly explained every single detail of the elimination episode. "I need to move again!"

We pant and puff our way up the long stone road, squeezing ourselves in between the masses of people enjoying their first morning under the open sky in days.

We dodge honking taxis, donkey carts, chattering families, and minibuses. We run through the capillary system of narrow alleys, past churches and mosques, through crowded bus stops and up the stone-paved roads, toward Manger Square. We run past walls painted with slogans in Arabic and English: *Just Peace! Freedom! Down with the Occupation!* We sprint alongside beautiful limestone villas and ostentatious colonial hotels and wave at other children playing in front of apartment buildings. We jump over the outstretched legs of men who sit on their doorsteps soaking up the sun as they caress their prayer beads or fiddle with their crosses. We run under and around clothes hanging on makeshift clotheslines. We run, and it feels good to feel the sun touch our faces, to feel the wind whip through our hair. Most of all, it feels good to hear life again.

Samy fights for me. He punches Khader in the gut. Khader returns with an uppercut, which Samy blocks.

"You sissy orphan!" Khader spits. "Defending a girl. A girl with a face like chopped meat."

Samy lunges at Khader's stomach headfirst.

Khader, who has a far more solid build, shoves Samy, who trips and falls to the ground. Khader raises his leg to kick him.

"Leave him alone!" I shout, slapping Khader's neck and crouching down to look at Samy.

Khader bursts into laughter. "Have him!" He walks off, clearly delighted with himself.

"Are you OK?" I ask Samy.

"No."

"Where does it hurt?"

Samy pulls himself up. "Hurt?" he repeats in an angry tone. "My reputation, *ya* Hayaat! Coming to my rescue. Oof! If I was bleeding like a cow in a butcher's shop, I would not want you to come to my rescue. All my credibility is gone now! Just leave me alone."

By lunchtime Samy has forgiven me because that is simply how it is with us. We can never stay angry with each other for long — there are too many things to do together. He steals an open can of paint from one of the classrooms and persuades Adham, Theresa, and me to join him at the section of the Wall that circles part of our school. Adham and Theresa harbor some doubts. Being associated with Samy often means getting into trouble with the teachers. The cane is never too far away either. But Samy knows how to dangle the carrot before the donkey. Accusing Adham of being a coward in front of Theresa, who has long silky hair and blue eyes, is enough to puff out Adham's chest and send him to the Wall, Theresa following out of curiosity.

As we approach, the concrete looms over us, absorbing us into an unnatural shade. The Wall snakes its way through the land, slicing through villages and cities, cutting families from each other, worshippers from their churches and mosques. The Wall scares me. I feel as though it will crush and suffocate me, even while it stands.

I look at the Wall and remember the day Rawya Amiry, the physiotherapist, lost her brother to it. This is what happens when I see the Wall. I see loss and death.

Rawya's eyes are so gray they are almost violet. She never wears makeup. Her hair is short and always slicked back with gel. (Mama used to consider her unfeminine but stopped talking negatively about Rawya after what happened. Rawya was suddenly promoted to the status of being one of the most beautiful women Mama has ever met, and Mama says that Rawya's hair, while short, is at least shiny.) When I returned home from school that day, I overheard Mama in the kitchen with Amto Samar. They were speaking in hushed tones as they chain-smoked, sipped sweetened coffee, and read their coffee grounds. I hid behind the door to listen to them, peeking through the gap in the slightly opened door.

"Rawya went to work," Mama said, adopting the quiet tone she reserves for woeful tales, "just like any other day. They say she massaged a woman's wrists and applied magnetic heat packs to a man with disc abnormalities. Perhaps she spoke about the weather or the peace talks or the best way to make cheesecake."

"She had no idea," Amto Samar lamented with a cluck of her tongue.

Mama blew a ring of smoke to the ceiling and took a sip of coffee. "She came home and found that her heart had been ripped out of her body and flattened with a bulldozer!"

"*Ya Allah!*"

"Her deaf and mute brother, Hisham, you know him, yes? Always seemed a little creepy, but of course that was because he could do nothing but stare, God have mercy on his soul."

"*Ameen,*" Amto Samar sang.

"He didn't stand a chance, *ya* Samar. The neighbors say they heard one of the soldiers shout out a warning through a loudspeaker. They tried to rush toward the driver of the bulldozer to tell him that Hisham was inside. But they were held back and Hisham was squashed into pieces, along with the rest of the house."

"God have mercy!"

I heard the click of the lighter and saw Amto Samar light another cigarette.

"I went with Foad and some of the others and searched through the rubble all night. Only parts of

Hisham's body were found. . . . His head was near the refrigerator."

Adham, Theresa, Samy, and I stand at the foot of the Wall, not far from a menacing watchtower. We're as small as ants.

"You first!" Samy says to Adham, motioning at the paint can and brush.

Adham suddenly looks reluctant. "What if we're caught?"

Samy smirks, folding his arms over his chest and flashing a glance at Theresa. "So what if we're caught? *I'm* not scared."

Adham raises an eyebrow and then snatches the brush and can of paint. He leans close to the Wall, his tongue slightly protruding as he frowns in concentration.

JESUS WEPPED.

"Ah!" Theresa exclaims. "I know that verse!"

Adham beams and Samy snatches the paintbrush from him.

"My turn now! I can write in English, too, you know!"

He starts to write: **FYT**

I step up beside Samy. *"F-I-G-H-T,"* I discreetly whisper into his ear. Before he can yell back at me, I rush on with my words: "And I am only telling you to save your credibility in front of Theresa."

Samy gives me a furious look, although I know he's secretly grateful. I grin and step back, enjoying his struggle to exercise self-restraint in front of Theresa, whom I suspect he likes given that he always tries to hold her hand during the *dabka*.

He quickly corrects the message and, when he finishes, steps back to admire his work.

FYTIGHT THE WALL UN TIL IT FOLLS

Theresa and Adham burst into laughter.

"Hey! What's so funny?"

"Nothing, Professor Samy," Adham says.

"Shut up, then!"

"I think it's very special," Theresa says in a sickly sweet voice.

"Then why are you laughing?" Samy snaps back, unable to hold his temper, even to the silky-haired Theresa.

She shrugs and his ears burn red.

"Just a silly girl," he says angrily.

"Don't you dare call me silly!"

"Stop shouting like a silly girl."

"You're stupid! And . . . and . . . you can't spell!"

She turns on her heel and storms off.

Adham chuckles but soon regrets it. Samy's fist swiftly comes in and connects with his shoulder.

"You humiliated me in front of Theresa, you idiot!"

I throw myself onto Samy and try to pry him off Adham.

"You're crazy!" Adham cries, rubbing his shoulder. "You should be locked up in Ktzi'ot Prison with your father!"

Fifteen minutes later Samy and I are sitting in the school office. Ostaza Mariam is with Adham, nursing his broken nose.

The principal, Ostaz Ihab, calls Samy in first. Ostaz Ihab stands at the door to his office, caressing his mustache as he clucks his tongue with disappointment. Samy, who's highly familiar with Ostaz Ihab and his cane, walks defiantly into the office and the door slams shut behind them.

A short while later Samy emerges, his hands red and raw. Ostaza Mariam walks past carrying a bloodied bandage in a plastic bag.

"Let me see your hands," she says tenderly, approaching Samy.

Samy quickly snatches his hands away and scowls at her. "I don't need your help," he shouts and runs out of the office.

Ostaz Ihab lectures me about playing with boys, avoiding troublemakers, and being more feminine. "You are a sweet girl," he says. "The girls are much better company for you."

I touch my face and stare at the frames decorating the wall behind his desk. Somebody has typed various popular songs and rhymes and framed them.

"Promise me you will make friends with the girls," he says. "Hayaat? Are you listening?"

"Yes, Ostaz," I say distractedly.

"Is that yes you are listening or yes you will promise?"

"Yes," I say.

FOUR

I wake up before God has granted the sun permission to rise.

Tariq has just kicked me in the face and mumbled that he has supernatural powers and will fly to America to eat a hamburger. I leave him with his dreams and shift my position. Then I notice Sitti Zeynab sitting up against her pillow, a round blue cookie tin perched on her lap.

"Why are you awake, Sitti?" I whisper, stumbling out of bed and sniffing the air as I sit beside her. I don't want to enter her personal zone with a fresh fart in the air, particularly as we ate fried cauliflower for dinner.

"Sleep would not come, my darling."

"What are you looking at?" I point to a photograph she is fondling in her frail, wrinkled hands, snuggling myself close beside her.

"Your grandfather. I miss him."

"I wish I'd met Sidi."

"You would have loved him. And he would have loved you. I am sure of it. He loved children. And his garden. And me." She flashes me a toothless grin and then casts a shy gaze at the photo.

"He had the eyes of a jinn —"

"A jinn!" The image is alarming.

"What do they teach you at school, those brainless donkeys? Did they not teach you that God made the jinn from fire, man from clay, and that the jinn worships God as man is supposed to? Just as there are wicked men, there are wicked jinn. And just as there are good men, there are good jinn. So he had the eyes of a good jinn, full of magic and dance. Among our friends he was called 'the smiling one.' He was so mischievous.

"One day I caught him in our garden with your uncle Saleem, God rest his soul. Saleem was young. I saw them through the kitchen window — I could see everything from that kitchen window, Hayaat. My village was perched high in the hills of Jerusalem and our house was at the top of the village. Through my kitchen window I saw your grandfather and Saleem crouching on the grass, their heads close together in some sort of conspiracy. Your grandfather's voice was loud and excitable. All of a sudden I heard Saleem scream. I ran outside. Your silly grandfather, God rest his soul, had been conducting an experiment with Saleem. Shall I tell you what it was? I am not a scientific woman, but I will never forget that experiment till the day I die. We spoke of it so often afterward."

"Yes, tell me!"

She rubs her hands together, clearly delighted with my enthusiasm.

"The two had dug a tiny hole in the ground. In it they put some water and covered it with an upside-down funnel. Then they threw some white powder that Saleem must have brought from school straight into the funnel. *Bang!* The stupid mixture exploded and the funnel hit Saleem in the forehead, leaving a bloody mark. They both dared to laugh hysterically! I chased Saleem all around the garden and when I caught him I gave him a big smack on the bum with all my might! The son of a donkey had given me a good fright! He could have been killed!"

"But it wasn't his fault! Sidi was helping him."

"Yes, I know," she says, her eyes twinkling. "So I chased him, too, and gave him a taste of a thrashing. But he could only laugh and declare that he was making a scientist out of Saleem!"

"Khalo Saleem *became* a scientist!"

A shadow passed over her face. "He died. . . ." she whispers. "I miss Jerusalem, Hayaat." Her voice is now so soft I can hardly hear it. "I try not to complain. I am in my daughter and son-in-law's home and your father has also lost his land. So I keep it inside, like he does." She clenches her fist and raises it to her heart.

"The nostalgia suffocates me. I see my limestone house in the village. I see the radio your grandfather bought when we went to the *souk* in the Old City. We kept the radio in the kitchen. I see the arched windows overlooking the hills, each window like a stone frame. I can smell my jasmine and almond trees and remember the olive trees I harvested. Those memories stow themselves in my windpipe until I dare not conjure another memory or I will scarcely be able to breathe.

"I am but six miles from Jerusalem and I am not allowed to enter it. Never again will I see the place where I was born, nor the home I entered as a bride. My olive trees, Hayaat. Oh, how I miss them! We had eleven, dotting the grounds around our house. You would have loved my home."

"What did it look like?"

"It was a two-story villa, made of beige limestone. Your grandfather and his father and his father's father were rich. The land had been in the family for generations. It was truly majestic. At the front was a small courtyard paved with a mosaic of black, green, and white tiles. On summer nights we brought our chairs and tables under the trees and sat with our friends, eating oranges and cooking *knafa* on a coal fire. I can still remember the scent of those trees.

"The front door was a brilliant burgundy, a white wrought-iron screen shielding it. The top of the door was carved into the shape of a crescent moon. There were two windows on either side of the door and they were arched, too, with colorful stained glass."

Although I've heard her stories many times I never tire of them.

"In that house I gave birth to Saleem, God rest his soul; and to Hany, God protect him, and God protect his Syrian wife with the big mouth and my three grandchildren. And I gave birth to Shams, God rest her soul. She died when she was just three, when we were living in the camp. And I gave birth to Ibtisam, God protect her and God protect her Palestinian husband and their children, who left our country to live in America, God grant them success. In the refugee camp I gave birth to Sharif, God protect him and his two children living in Australia, at the end of the earth! Oh, why could they not have had four or five children? And God rest his wife's soul and forgive me for any negative words I may have said about her in the past for taking him to the ends of the earth, and, finally I gave birth to your mother, God protect —"

"Sitti?"

"Yes, Hayaat?"

"Can I make a suggestion? Why don't you name all your children and then say a general prayer? It would speed things up for you."

"Eh? Do not be silly."

I sigh impatiently and wait for her prayer ramblings to finish.

"How did you lose your home?" I quickly ask. I've

heard the story countless times, but it's worth hearing it again if only to distract her before she prays for half of the West Bank.

She throws her veil over her face and starts to moan. I gently lower her veil, and she raises her eyes to the ceiling.

"It was 1948. There was fighting everywhere. We were terrified of the *Irgun* and the *Haganah*." These were Zionist organizations that fought for a Jewish state. "We were so afraid. Every day news would come of more victims, of villagers being terrorized and forced to leave their homes. We heard of the nearby village of Deir Yassin. Two hundred of its men, women, and children were massacred, Hayaat. Can you imagine our fear? The armed forces came and drove us out. We took what we could carry on our backs. It never occurred to us that we would not return. We locked the doors. Imagine that . . . ?" I'm hooked and beg her to continue.

"The State of Israel was declared soon after. I didn't see my home again until after 1967." She sighs dramatically, raising her eyes to the ceiling again. "In 1950 they passed a new law. Anybody who was not in Israel on

September 1, 1948, was declared a *present absentee* owner. Huh! Have your teachers taught you about that law?"

"No."

"What they teach you, I don't understand! Well, the law means *khara*."

"You swore!"

"God forgive me." She mutters a prayer under her breath and asks me to place a pillow behind her back. Despite the heat, she requests I drape a blanket over her shoulders. She peers at Jihan and Tariq, lying comatose on the bed, and then sighs. "The law says that all our property could now be leased or sold."

"I hate them!"

Sitti Zeynab knits her eyebrows. "We Arabs say that the wound that bleeds inwardly is the most dangerous. So I do not hate, *ya* Hayaat. It will not return my land to me."

I frown. "But it's not fair."

She takes my chin in her hand and looks me in the eye. "I say this to you because you are the daughter of my daughter. Feel as you wish, that is your right. But you will soon find that even hatred will not give you comfort. It will only make you miserable.

"It is a funny world, *ya* Hayaat. Oh, I know I am as old as a mountain, but I have learned some strange things along the way." She pauses and then excitedly rummages through her tin. "Here, look!"

"What is it?"

"The deeds to my land," she whispers, as though letting me in on a special secret.

She scrunches up her wrinkled nose and her face suddenly erupts into anger. "My home was occupied! Stolen! So many times, *ya* Hayaat, did I wonder, after we fled, what happened to our belongings. Were our furniture and our clothes and my pots and pans being used? Or had it all been thrown out? I could never decide which was worse.

"We lost our friends and family. There was no time for good-bye. We fled, thinking we would return days or weeks later. I remember the nights in the camp when we would all gather to listen to the radio, to the messages from people in other camps. Ooh! Our ears would perk up like rabbits, waiting for a message from somebody we knew.

"We only ever heard a message from one person we knew: your grandfather's cousin. Your aunt Ibtisam was a baby then. She had terrible wind but I was busy feeding Shams. Shams was sickly since the day she was born and always hungry. So your grandfather sat with me in our tent as I instructed him to put warm olive oil in Ibtisam's belly button."

"What?"

"It is soothing." Ignoring my dropped jaw, she continues: "As he slowly poured drops of the oil over Ibtisam's belly, we heard the radio presenter say: 'Abu Nasser Mahmoud Abdel-Razak says that he is safe with his family in Shatila camp in northern Lebanon.' Your grandfather was so shocked he forgot what he was doing and nearly poured the entire jar over Ibtisam!" Her heavy shoulders vibrate as she chuckles quietly. "Then he started to sob. I tell you, Hayaat, men have never, and will never, know how to do two things at once. I was crying, too, but I still managed to nurse Shams. But your grandfather could not handle sobbing for Abu Nasser and attending to a wailing Ibtisam, who, by the way, was now as greasy as a marinated chicken. So he slipped Ibtisam into my arms and I tried to soothe her, feed Shams, and cry for Abu Nasser all at the same time."

"When did you see your home again, Sitti?"

"After the Six Days' War. Sometime in 1967 we returned. What was once my village was now classified as West Jerusalem. Many of the homes were now occupied by Israeli families. Some parts had changed, so much so that they were unrecognizable to us. Your grandfather and I, along with Hany, Ibtisam, God protect Saleem —"

"Yes, yes!" I interrupt impatiently. "God rest their souls and open the heavens to them and everyone they have ever encountered in their lives. So, about your return? What happened?"

"I am old and forget where I put my slippers and when your mother's birthday is, but know this, *ya* Hayaat: That day is burned into my memory. I can remember every detail.

"Saleem didn't come with us, for he was working in Kuwait then, so Hany and Ibtisam, who were now grown-up, did. Hany was working for an Israeli family near Netanya, so he spoke Hebrew and could translate. Your mother was seven and Sharif was nine but they were very naughty and so I left them in the care of a friend. We walked through the village and I heard the silence of my people, Hayaat. They were like ghosts, hovering around us. As we walked the wide village streets and the narrow alleys that had not been destroyed, I felt like an orphan who, after many years, is reunited with her parents.

"We walked past the site of the village mosque, which was also used as a club. Houses for the new Israeli population had been built over it. I remembered how we congregated at the mosque's entrance during Eid, parading ourselves in our new Eid clothes, the children comparing how much money they had been given from their families. Sheep would be slaughtered to commemorate Prophet Abraham's sacrifice and the feast would last through the evening.

"Your grandfather wanted to pray two *raka'a* on the street, but I would not let him. I was afraid it would cause trouble.

"We ascended a small incline and saw our house. Time had stood still; the exterior had not changed. We arrived at the gate that led into the courtyard. It was ajar, so your grandfather pushed it open and we walked in. 'Stay here,' your grandfather said, his voice shaky. But I refused. I had to see my home again. Hany and Ibtisam, one on each arm, steadied me. We walked over the tiles and approached the three steps to the front door. We were suddenly excited, exchanging memories, competing for Ibtisam's attention as we sought to bring to life the house she had been born in.

"Then the front door flew open and standing there, on my doorstep, under *my* roof, was a man with blue eyes and pale skin. He wore a long black coat but his feet were bare. I think back about that now and it brings a smile to my face. The man must have dressed in such a hurry that he had forgotten to put shoes on. His bare feet peeked out from under his gown."

As Sitti Zeynab speaks, I feel myself there, perched in an almond tree in the courtyard, watching the scene unfold.

"'Get off my property!' he ordered us, shooing us away. It was almost comical, Hayaat. We could not even converse with each other. Hany translated for us, but it was clear from his tone that we were being ordered away.

"Your grandfather gasped. I will never forget that sound, like the man's words were hands choking your grandfather's neck. And then a woman appeared next to him. She was beautiful, her neck long and white, her eyes sky blue. She was skinny and petite and was wearing a green apron that was stained with flour and oil. I am not a violent person, *ya habibti*, but I swear to God that at that moment I wanted to gouge her eyes out as I imagined her cooking in my kitchen, looking out of *my* window, using my stove and my shelves.

"Hany rushed to your grandfather's side and Ibtisam gripped me tight. And then the woman spoke. 'This is our land,' Hany translated. Her voice was shaky and nervous, like a hesitant child clutching on to a toy she knows does not belong to her. Later that night, when I lay waiting for sleep to come over me, I thought about words, theirs and ours, and how useless they can be.

"'It is our land!' your grandfather declared in Arabic, taking the title deeds out of the pocket of his brown *galabiya*. These deeds I hold now. The man and woman looked at us, puzzled. Your grandfather adjusted the red-and-white *keffiyeh* over his head, something he did when he was nervous, as Hany translated his words. I took the key out of my pocket and held it up for them to see. The man puffed his chest up and, turning to

Hany, said that our title deeds meant nothing now. He said we had abandoned our home and the State of Israel had seized it. He said it was now their property and we were trespassing. I wanted to weep but could not allow them the satisfaction.

"I tried to reason with them. 'Hany, tell them this is our home,' I said. 'Tell them we were forced out, but we were coming back. Ask them what right they have to our home!' The woman tried to explain. She said that she had lost her family in the Nazi concentration camps. Her mother, her father, and her twin sister. They were gassed, Hayaat.

"I was confused. I took a step forward, pleading with the woman to understand. Through Hany I responded: 'I'm sorry for what happened to your family and your people, but why must we be punished?'

"'The State of Israel has been declared,' the woman's husband said, 'and the past is the past. So forget your home for it is now ours. Go to Egypt or Jordan or Syria. You have many countries from which to choose.' He actually looked pleased with himself when he made this suggestion. As though he was making a conciliatory gesture. 'But this is our homeland!' Hany cried. 'Would you ask an Englishman to move to America or Australia because they speak English in those countries too? Palestine is our home, not Egypt or Syria.' We kept arguing, Hany standing in the middle, until the man turned and went inside. He came back out with a gun. 'Get off our land,' he ordered. I was pathetic, Hayaat. In my terror I screamed like a child and felt instant shame. Ibtisam pulled me toward the street, yelling out at your grandfather and Hany to move away.

"We tried, *ya habibti*, but it was no good, our fate was sealed. The camp was the only home we had now."

I lower my head against Sitti Zeynab's shoulder. This is the first time Sitti Zeynab has spoken so openly about how she became a refugee. Her story chills me. Having lost our home in Beit Sahour, I feel like I know exactly what she went through.

Her voice is barely a whisper now as I lose her to her memories. "I was in the refugee camp when I heard their woman prime minister, I can't remember her name, say: 'There were no such things as Palestinians. They did not exist.' I went to bed that night with a fever. Her words poisoned me, Hayaat. I existed, *ya* Hayaat. I exist!"

I pat her hand, trying to calm her.

"If I could have one wish, Hayaat, it would be to touch the soil of my home one last time before I die. Land, *ya* Hayaat. There is nothing so important. The deeper your roots, the taller and stronger you grow. When your roots are ripped out from under you, you risk shriveling up. All I want is to die on my land. Not in my daughter's home, but in *my* home."

I reach out my hands and touch her lined face. Pools of moonlight find their way through spaces in the curtains and throw shadows across her face, a chaotic map of intersecting wrinkles. Her eyes are a deep hazel and shine out from under the white of her veil, which is draped loosely around her head and shoulders out of habit. Strands of silvery, fair hair fall down the sides of her face. She smiles at me and again rummages through the tin, retrieving a large iron skeleton key. It hangs from the tassel of a black scarf.

"The key to my home." She sighs deeply and then smiles. "I took it with me when we fled. I tucked it into my undergarments. It itched against my skin as we ran but I knew I had to keep it with me — for when we returned. . . . The tent was our new home. Eventually, when we realized we would never be allowed to return or even be compensated, we understood that the camp was permanent. And then, when your grandfather died —"

"Of a broken and crushed heart?" Even though I had heard the story many times, Sitti Zeynab had never fully explained my grandfather's death. Did my grandfather suffer the way Baba was now suffering?

"He was run over by a car."

"Oh." I need to know Baba's reaction is normal. I ask her again.

"But was his heart broken?"

"Yes, of course it was," she says, looking confused. "And every other part of his body. It was a big car."

I refrain from rolling my eyes and change the subject. "When did you move in with Mama?"

"Your mother married your father and I was glad. Because your father had land, olive groves, and a nice laugh."

"A nice laugh?" I say in disbelief. "I never hear it."

"Your father has had bad things happen to him.

And he is sad. So maybe it is not so surprising that you do not hear his nice laugh that often. We can't all be like your grandfather. He could find happiness anywhere. That is the fortune of people who have simple hearts. How I envy them. Mine was filled with bitterness and anger. We were fed by United Nations workers and it hurt my pride. I hated the Arab countries, the traitors. I hated Israelis. I hated the United Nations. I hated the West. I hated the East. I hated lining up like a beggar for food for my family when I had once had a two-story home with arched windows and tiles.

"'Give thanks to God we are alive,' your grandfather would tell me. I was not religious then. I had planned to leave religion until I was white-haired and ugly, fool that I was. But I was a beauty, Hayaat. Did you know I had yellow hair?" She twirls a piece of her hair around her finger. "See," she says, thrusting it in front of my eyes, "it is so light."

"But I thought you said the one-eyed is a beauty in the land of the blind?"

"Oh, but even the blind could have sensed the lightness of my hair, Hayaat."

I hold back a giggle.

"Your grandfather's attitude frustrated me at times. I was living in a tent, freezing in winter and sweating away with the flies in summer. But I had had a home once. Yes, with tiles and high ceilings and furniture. It's like heartburn after a big meal. It burns inside and nothing you do takes the sensation away."

I tilt my head to the side. "A glass of milk?"

"Huh! They would even deny me that!"

"You can buy it from any shop. Abu Yusuf sells it."

Sitti Zeynab rolls her eyes and speaks to the ceiling. "This is why the constant closure of schools is such a crime. Metaphorical language is lost on our youth."

I don't bother responding.

"I thought about a lot of things in that camp, Hayaat. And since then I have not stopped thinking. They do not have two heads and ten feet."

"Who? The refugees?"

"No, the Israelis. That is the saddest part of it all. That woman who stole my home must have also kissed and played with her children. She must have also dreamed and loved. Like me she knew pain and suffering and the torment of losing one's family and home.

"I remember bumping into one of our neighbors from the village when we were in the food line at the camp. He was a sour man who used to hit his children. I once sent your grandfather to stop him, for the children's cries were tormenting me. We exchanged glances in the line and he shoved his son forward, as though he were a beast to tame. I realized then that even those capable of love and kindness can be unjust. And even those who are the victims of injustice can be cruel and incapable of love."

"Do you think they laugh?" I ask after a moment of silence.

She pauses, fondling the key in her hand. "Yes, of course they do. I see them on the television beside the Mediterranean in Tel Aviv, sun-baking in their bathing suits — God forgive their immodesty — playing ball games and laughing under the sun. Yes, Hayaat. They laugh. It is just that nobody has realized that laughter sounds the same, whether it shakes its way out of an Israeli or a Palestinian."

FIVE

The next morning Sitti Zeynab wakes up, eats half a boiled egg, and then collapses onto the floor.

"Mama! Help!" I shriek, throwing myself onto Sitti Zeynab's motionless body, yelling out to her to wake up.

Mama runs into the living room and screams. "Foad! Foad! Mama has collapsed!"

Mama tries to pry me off Sitti Zeynab, but I won't budge.

"Let me check if there is a pulse!" she cries, finally dragging me off. I sit crumpled beside them, sobbing as I watch Mama place her fingers on Sitti Zeynab's wrist.

"Please, please, please," I keep repeating in a low voice. Tariq and Jihan rush into the room. Tariq starts screaming and Jihan tries to muffle him by engulfing him in her arms. But he can't be silenced; his wails rise to the ceiling.

"There is a pulse!" Mama yells. "It is faint!"

We hear Baba's footsteps crashing down on the stairs from the roof. He rushes into the room. "What is wrong?"

He bounds across the room, shouting out orders in a controlled voice. "Jihan, call the ambulance. Hayaat, take Tariq to your room and calm him."

"No!" My refusal leaps out of my mouth so quickly that I'm as shocked as Baba. He looks at me in stunned silence. "I'm not leaving her," I cry. Then I burst into a fresh flow of tears and he lets me be.

The ambulance arrives shortly afterward.

"See how God favors her?" Mama says as the EMTs carefully lift Sitti Zeynab from the floor and place her on a stretcher. "There is no curfew. She is one of God's loved ones — and I was short-tempered with her this morning when she asked me to remake her tea because it had gone cold. God forgive me!" Mama covers her face with her hands and starts to sob. Baba sighs but doesn't approach her. It's no longer their habit to be tender with each other.

The EMTs load Sitti Zeynab into the ambulance. Baba insists we sit on the front steps and not disturb them. Tariq sits beside me, biting his nails and staring intently at the ambulance.

"I want to hear the siren," he whispers in my ear shyly. "Could you ask them to turn it on?"

"Mama will be angry," I say in a distracted tone.

He seems to think about this for a moment. "Yes. But it's worth it."

Jihan hitches Mohammed up on her hip and surveys the scene. Mama yells out orders faster than bullets shot from a machine gun: "Keep Mohammed warm. Feed him the formula milk on the top of the stove. Change his diaper and apply cream. Actually, no, I will take him with me, otherwise it will be too difficult. It is best not to leave the house today except for school. Don't fight. Defrost the chicken in cold water, but don't waste water. Tell the neighbors, but not Um Amjad for she has a meddling heart and will cast the black eye on us. Stay out of trouble."

I leave Jihan and Mama to negotiate the terms of Jihan's position of authority over us (her word is law until my parents return) and approach Sitti Zeynab, who lies motionless on the stretcher in the ambulance. The beginnings of a plan are swimming around in my head. I need to see Sitti Zeynab one last time. To know if I will have the courage to go ahead with my plan.

The two EMTs look frazzled and smile wearily at me. "We must leave now," they say in urgent tones.

"I won't be long," I reassure them and jump up onto the back of the ambulance, kneeling over Sitti Zeynab. I press my lips close to her right ear. I want to say something so profound that she wakes up. But my mind is numb. All I can do is remember the walk we took through her memories the night before.

"Stay alive," I whisper. "I'll let you touch that soil again." She doesn't stir.

I kiss her wrinkled cheek and jump out of the ambulance.

I'm on a mission now. And I desperately need a partner.

SIX

Samy and I are walking to school, through what was once a wide residential street. This side of the street is lined with beautiful houses made of limestone. The courtyards that lead to white and bottle-green wrought-iron front doors are large and filled with palm and fern trees, their foliage leaning over the walls and creating pockets of shade on the street. High green, black, and white gates mark the entrance to each house.

No more than ten feet across from the gates stands the Wall, cutting the once wide street in half. The only view the houses have on this side is a dark assembly of vertical concrete panels that tower twenty-five feet high. A tall, circular watchtower is constructed at a section of the Wall and it aligns with the last house in the street. The watchtower has three rectangular slits positioned side by side, slanting eyes in a face of gray. Split in half, there is no street name visible on this side. Perhaps it has fallen on the other side. The name and named are now divorced.

Samy pauses before one of the houses, fascinated by a huge tree he has spotted. One of its branches hangs over a large retaining wall, and he leaps into the air, grabs the branch with both hands, and pulls himself up. He then straddles the branch, looking pleased with himself. I am transfixed by the concrete panels of the Wall. I can't tell where the sky ends and where the Wall begins.

"Will she be OK?" Samy asks.

"I don't know. But I know what will make her better."

I tell him about my plan to visit Sitti Zeynab's village and bring back some soil from her land. I'm afraid that he'll tell me I'm being stupid, just like a girl, so I don't dare meet his eyes as I speak. When I finish I look up. He is silent for a moment, tapping his hands against the branch.

"I'll go with you."

"Really?"

"We've got algebra with Ostaz Hany tomorrow. He has the breath of a dead sheep and insists on breathing down your neck when you do your work. Why would I go to school? But I have to be home before dark because Amo Joseph is forcing me to go to church with him tomorrow night. Father Anthony's just returned from Ramallah so he's holding a special mass."

"Is it as boring as prayers at the mosque?"

He looks at me as though that's a stupid question. "He numbs my brain. My uncle can see that I don't pay attention and clips me on the ear every two minutes. I'm actually grateful because it keeps me awake."

"I close my eyes during prayers, and when Mama accuses me of lacking faith, I tell her that closing my eyes brings me closer to Allah. She beams."

"Father Anthony always preaches to us about being strong in the face of oppression. 'Never give in or be a coward against the Zionist occupation,' he says. But then I saw him forced to strip down to his undergarments at a checkpoint one day! Where was his courage then?" He screws his face up in disgust and then jumps down off the branch. "His chest hair was white! I couldn't bear to see him like that. A priest! With his white chest hair curling in the wind for the soldiers to laugh at! How many times have I told you, Hayaat, the grown-ups are no use? They can't protect us or themselves." He shakes his head and hits his forehead. "*Yaa!* I forgot. How will we get to Jerusalem? We're not allowed in!"

"It's only about six miles away."

"Are you mad? We'll never make it."

I've forgotten about this detail. We're two children from Bethlehem, and I'd forgotten that Jerusalem is forbidden to us for as long as we live.

I lower my head, disappointment flooding my body. I caress the scars on my cheek, staring down at the ground.

"Of course, we could always try to enter through the back roads," Samy says.

"You mean *illegally*?"

He nods thoughtfully. "We'll find people who have been turned away at the checkpoints and are taking the back roads. People do it all the time ... don't they?"

I shrug. "I don't know."

"I think they do. We'll need to take a service taxi. And if we're turned away at the checkpoints, we'll sneak around, somehow. I'm sure it can be managed."

"What if we die?"

"Eh?"

"What if we get shot?"

"I probably won't. I have my cross for protection. I can lend you one if you like. But you're Muslim so it might not work."

I giggle. "Yeah, probably not."

"Anyway, you'll be a martyr."

I don't like the idea. Once, when my face was normal, I used to think it was all very well to die for freedom, peace, justice, and so on. But it would have to be spectacular, I thought. Like throwing oneself in front of a tank to protect an old man. Sometimes I'd fall into a daydream, usually after Mama or Baba had scolded me and I wanted to punish them by dying and making them feel guilty, and I'd imagine that I had died in heroic circumstances and my parents and school were all consumed with grief. People would chant my name, and women would faint with distress, and my family would gather around and share stories about me. They would say that I lived like an angel, and they would have conveniently forgotten all the times I was clipped on the ear for not making my bed or refusing to eat okra. I would feel my chest swell as I imagined all the nice things they would say about me.

Now, however, I know a courageous death is nice in theory only.

"I would rather live," I say.

"Me too. So we'll try our very best not to get shot. Don't wear that awful pink-and-red dress you insist on blinding everyone's eyes with. My cross will only work so far."

"I love that dress."

He rolls his eyes. "Even a cockeyed trainee soldier would spot you in that dress. We need money for the transport," he adds.

"My parents have a stash hidden in my father's underwear drawer. I'll borrow some after they leave to go to the hospital tomorrow. It's for a good cause. And I'll borrow some from Jihan. She's been saving her money to buy an exercise machine."

"She'll kill you."

"I know."

"I have a little money, too, and I can always steal some from Amto Christina's charity tin. Helping Sitti Zeynab counts as charity. So what do we put the soil in?"

I rummage through my schoolbag and retrieve an empty hummus jar.

"Good idea. But you've got my stomach rumbling now. *Yallah*, let's buy a sandwich from George's Bakery before school starts!"

Mama and Baba come home later that night without Sitti Zeynab. Baba immediately heads to the kitchen to prepare his *argeela*. Mama drops into a chair. Her legs are outstretched and she clasps an unlit cigarette in her hand. She leans her head back and closes her eyes, releasing a weary sigh.

"Well? Mama, is she OK?"

"Yes," Mama says without opening her eyes. "It's just old age, *habibti*. Her heart is getting weaker. God keep her with us. She'll be home tomorrow, *inshallah*, God willing."

I sit on the edge of the couch and bite my nails. Relief floods through me. The scary things — stroke, heart attack, cancer — have been ruled out, thank God. But the fragility of Sitti Zeynab's health still terrifies me.

I go to my room. Jihan is busy doing lunges in the corner and singing to her Walkman. I get a piece of paper and write down the name of Sitti Zeynab's village and her description of her home. I tuck it into the Shrek backpack Baba got me as a present. I check that the empty hummus jar is secure and decide to wrap it in one of Mohammed's blankets to cushion it properly. I've packed some snacks for the journey. My birth certificate is folded in an envelope, secured in the front pocket of the bag.

I go to bed early. I dream of tanks chasing me down the streets of Jerusalem. I dream I've been buried alive. Maysaa scoops dirt over me, but I can't scream because my mouth is full of rocks and compost. I wake up in a cold sweat. I look over at Sitti Zeynab's empty bed and realize just how much I need her. I force myself to close my eyes and replay the words of a pop song in my head until I fall asleep.

SEVEN

I leave the house early the next morning. I write Jihan a note telling her I've gone to school. She lies snoring beside Tariq; none of us even contemplated sleeping in Sitti Zeynab's empty bed.

Samy and I have no idea how to get to Jerusalem and so we agree to head to the main service taxi stand at Manger Square.

Bethlehem hasn't fully woken yet. Many of the tourists with their astonished and wonder-filled eyes who walk the stone streets of the holy town are probably still snuggled fast asleep in their hotel beds. They come in their jeans, walking shoes, T-shirts, and baseball caps. Sports bags perched on their backs, cameras dangling off straps around their necks, they're eager to experience the place where Jesus was born. Samy and I like to watch them as they listen eagerly to their

Palestinian tour guide, who happily explains the history behind the Church of Nativity and leads them to souvenir shops where they can purchase mugs, T-shirts, paintings, or mouse pads with prints of the Virgin Mary holding a baby Jesus (all at a special commission to the tour guide, Baba says).

Samy and I enjoy talking to the tourists. They're either overwhelmed (in which case we feel sorry for them and will shoo the beggars and child merchants away) or excited (in which case we pose in photos with them and practice our English skills on them).

As we're walking, we're surprised to overhear two men in loud conversation. Samy grins at me and cries out to them: "We speak London too!"

Laughing, I grab Samy's arm and pull him away.

"People don't speak London, silly!" I say.

"Well, what was that, then?"

"It's an *English* accent. They were speaking *English*."

"London, English, it's the same thing."

"You need to stop sleeping in Ostaza Mariam's classes."

"OK, teacher's pet."

We start to kick a smooth gray pebble, taking turns in passing it to each other as we walk along the street. Then we get into another argument, which we often do. It all starts when I tell Samy that I want to be a vet and zookeeper when I grow up. He snorts and then asks me what kind of zoo.

"A zoo where people can walk around with the animals."

This seems to amuse him very much. "You can't have a zoo without cages. People would get eaten by the animals."

"No, they wouldn't. I would train the animals to be gentle."

"You can't tame a lion to take a stroll with a human. Don't be ridiculous."

"You can so!" I shout, infuriated by his cynicism. "There are places in the world where people observe animals close up! They're called *safaris*."

"Safaris? It's *sarafis*, silly."

"It is not."

"Yes, it is."

"Is not."

"Is too."

"No."

"Yes. *Sarafi! Sarafi! Sarafi!*"

"Oh, shut up."

"Anyway, what are you talking about? And stop talking as though you have any idea what's out in the world. You've never even seen a lion. Or a monkey. Not even a camel. And we're in the Middle East for God's sake!"

I kick the pebble hard and far, sending him running to kick it farther. The rule is that the first person to miss the next kick loses. And neither one of us likes to lose.

"I've seen them on television!"

"And that's how you'll become the first Palestinian lion tamer?" He doubles over with an exaggerated laugh and then kicks the pebble, forcing me to retrieve it from a tricky angle in the gutter.

"I'll obviously study for the position," I say, managing to kick the pebble a short distance.

"Study where? There are no courses."

I stop in front of him, placing my hands furiously on my hips. "You donkey, that's what universities are for!"

"Well, the animals won't be able to get through the checkpoints. Can you imagine an elephant begging a soldier to let him pass? Your idea is stupid. And you're not such an animal-loving person after all. You just called me a donkey!"

"Oh, shut up. Anyway, my idea's not stupid! I'll write to people around the world and they'll send the animals and the Israelis will say yes."

"Why?" he asks, a sneer on his face. "Because they like animals more than they like us?"

I shrug my shoulders. "They'll say yes. And I'll open the first zoo without cages. And it'll be open for everybody! Except you!"

He gives me an angry look. "Stop dreaming stupid dreams."

"It's not a stupid dream!"

"Yes, it is!"

We've suddenly forgotten all about the pebble.

"Well, what do you want to be, then? Huh?"

He frowns. "What's the point of wanting to be anything?"

I throw my hands in the air in exasperation. "Are

you saying you wouldn't want to be a doctor? A shop owner? A truck driver? A teacher?"

"A teacher? Hayaat, you must be crazy! Imagine if I had to teach somebody like me. I would have a nervous breakdown the way Ostaz Shady nearly did after I superglued his briefcase closed. And a doctor? Too much blood. A shop owner? People are poor, so what's the point? A truck driver? Why? So it can get confiscated like Abdullah's did? Or so I can spend every day driving from checkpoint to roadblock? No thank you. I don't dream stupid dreams, Hayaat."

For a moment I don't say anything. I stare into his eyes. "I don't believe you," I whisper.

He holds my stare and then grins. "Does wanting to be a soccer player count?"

I offer him a shrug. "Maybe."

"Well, that's what I want to be. And when your cageless zoo idea fails, you can always come to me and I'll employ you as my personal assistant. You can manage my fan mail and advertising contracts."

I dive at him but he's too quick, stepping to the side and erupting into a fit of laughter.

We press on toward the center of Bethlehem. The marketplace is already noisy and chaotic, even at this early hour. We dodge the taxis and cars that race through the streets, somehow negotiating their way through pedestrians, fruit stands, ambling donkeys, broken footpaths, and redundant traffic islands. Shop owners stand outside their shops, smoking as they lean against their doors, surveying the scene with bored expressions. Children run after their mothers and fathers carrying shopping bags and cartons of fruit and vegetables. We run in front of an overcrowded bus and wave at the passengers. We run past the Armenian Convent and down Milk Grotto Street with its numerous souvenir shops selling silver jewelry and handmade crucifixes, medals, rosaries, and boxes carved from olive wood and decorated with mother-of-pearl. We run past restaurants, cafés, and bars, where men sit at the entrances haggling and gossiping over small cups of Turkish coffee. Finally we reach Manger Square. I crouch down and lean my head between my legs, trying to calm my shuddering breath.

Now that we're here, I decide I want to pay a quick visit to the Mosque of Omar, which stands at the edge of Manger Square.

Samy is incredulous. "Are you joking?" he splutters. "Why?"

"I won't be long. I promise."

As we approach the mosque we're greeted by an old man who's sucking on a cigarette. He looks us up and down, a goofy grin on his face.

"Give alms for the martyred ones!" he cries, shaking a tin of money in his crusty old hand. His red gums are laid bare for us to see as he laughs boisterously. It's obvious that he's not right in the head.

"Give alms for those who fight the Israelis!" he cries, shaking his tin.

I ignore him, averting my eyes from his as I scurry past. I approach the women's entrance, Samy following me. Samy then stops, kisses his cross, and mutters, "God forgive me."

"You have to enter through the men's entrance," I say, pointing him in its direction. "I'll meet you inside."

We separate and I grab a scarf from a clothing rack and throw it over my hair.

I meet up with Samy and we pick a corner of the mosque, careful to avoid eye contact with a group of men sitting in a circle.

I kneel down on the carpet and raise my palms in front of my face and make *dua*. *Please keep her with us. Please keep her alive. Please help us at the checkpoints.*

"Amto Christina wouldn't be impressed if she knew I was here," Samy mutters. "Wait for a moment. I need to go to the bathroom. . . . I'll be back." He bolts out of the door.

Several moments later a girl in a green *hijab* crouches down beside me. I turn to face her, curious as to why she's chosen to sit beside me when she has the entire mosque. Grinning at me, his teeth practically luminous under the lights in the mosque, is Samy, draped in the green *hijab*. He bats his eyelashes at me and forces back a hysterical laugh.

"Are you crazy?" I hiss.

"No," he whispers. "I just want to see if anybody notices."

"You're the ugliest girl I've ever seen. Praise God for making you a boy. I never realized how big your nostrils were until now. And your eyebrows — there's only one."

"Was it always like that?"

"They've warmed the top of your nose ever since I can remember. Come on, let's leave. I'm finished."

I grab his arm and lead him out, away from the curious eyes of the men, who, judging from the steady hum of conversation from the direction of their circle, seem to be enjoying a gossip session rather than a religious lecture.

As we step out of the mosque, I notice a small boy who looks our age talking to the old man. Upon seeing us, the old man whispers something into the boy's ear, and the boy runs after us, cutting off our path. A plastic bag filled with packets of tissues dangles from his arm. His hair is disheveled and dusty, the heels of his shoes run-down, and his clothes are ragged and too big for him.

"Tissues?" he asks. "May God give you a long life."

"Go away," Samy says, although he says it without

much energy. It's a standard response to street hagglers and the boy doesn't even flinch. "Do we look like tourists? Leave us alone, we've got important business."

The boy's eyes light up. "My uncle thought you looked suspicious."

"That crazy man is your uncle?" Samy says.

"Yeah. So what business do you have?" He licks his lips in anticipation of Samy's response.

"We are on a private mission," Samy replies importantly.

"Tell me," the boy pleads. Then he looks at me. I'm twirling the end of my braid on my finger, thinking about how dirty his skin is.

"Where are you from?" I ask. We start to walk and the boy follows us.

"My uncle and I are from Aida refugee camp. Are you from there too?"

"Certainly not!" I cry with indignation. That Mama was born in a refugee camp and lived there until she was married isn't something I like to advertise. For some reason, seeing this scruffy, starved-looking boy makes me angry. "Why don't you wash?" I ask scornfully. "I'm sure there's soap in the camp. You smell! And your clothes are filthy."

The boy shrugs. "Tell me about your *mission*. I'm bored."

"Go away," I say, flicking my hand in the air as though I'm trying to get rid of a fly. "We don't have time for you."

"Why is your face like that? What happened to you? Does it hurt?"

I turn around swiftly and glare at him. "Shut up! Leave me alone, you filthy, stinking refugee!"

His eyes suddenly moisten. He makes as if to tie his shoelace. But his shoes don't have laces. The shame I feel in that moment floods my body with such force I feel as though I might topple over. To think that somebody has to protect their self-respect and dignity from me. After all the teasing I've endured at school. After all the times I've looked in the mirror and felt embarrassed by my reflection.

I buy his entire bag of tissues.

"What are we going to do with all those tissues?" Samy asks as he watches me stuff the small packets into my backpack.

"What we do with them isn't the point," I mutter.

"I saw an episode of *Batman*," the boy says thought-fully, "where he rescues someone who tries to climb up a building with bedsheets tied together."

Samy is interested.

"Imagine if you tied the tissues together and climbed the walls of the Old City."

"Imagine if the soldiers saw us doing that," Samy says with a laugh. "I think they'd let us in to reward our pure genius."

"A tissue crumples with a bit of snot and you two think it's going to carry our body weight?"

"Where's your imagination?" the boy asks, giving Samy a knowing look.

"She's being Miss Practical today," Samy says.

"Come on, let's get moving," I say. "If you both shut up, I'll show you the kite I have stuffed in my bag. We'll get Batman here to hold it over the Wall while you and I dangle off the ribbons, Samy. Now *yallah*. We need to find out how to get to Jerusalem."

EIGHT

The dirty boy from Aida refugee camp who has no tissues left to sell is named Wasim. We let him walk with us because he's been recruited by a United Nations–sponsored soccer team to play in international tournaments. Samy is instantly impressed. I don't know whether he wants to embrace Wasim or hit him.

"Why you?" Samy asks, his voice dripping with envy. "How did you get picked? I mean, you're a refugee."

Wasim grins. "That's the point, *ya zalami.*" I can't help but snort in laughter. *Ya zalami* means "man," but only old people say such things. It sounds funny coming out of Wasim's mouth. "Because I'm a refugee, they took pity. I'm going to be trained. Actual training! With real soccer cleats and jerseys and knee pads!"

"Knee pads?" Samy's eyes are as big as the saucers Mama uses to serve *mansaf.* "Huh! Liar."

"I swear to God, *ya zalami.* And the coach is from England with an accent and everything!"

"*Englizee?*"

"*Ya zalami,* he drinks more tea than we do!"

"Stop lying!"

"I promise on my mother's grave. The foreigners came to Aida camp with an idea to help the kids, and they saw we love to play soccer and decided to sponsor a team. It was just a tiny bit of their budget. And *Wallah,* I swear to God, I would rather have soccer than food. So do you want to play? Practice with me? We could do it every week. Every day, even!"

Wasim's been promoted to hero status. The two of them are boring me with their inane sports talk. I huff and puff, but they're oblivious.

"Where will you play?" I ask eventually, conceding defeat.

Wasim jumps up and punches the air. "In Italy!"

Samy is clearly distressed. He stops, shuffles along, and then stops again, grabbing Wasim's arm. "Well, can't you . . . ask them to let me play too? I'm excellent! Hayaat, tell him how excellent I am. Tell him. Go on. Tell him!"

"He's terrible," I say. In a split second, I realize that if I don't correct myself, Samy will die. He's losing his coloring and the oxygen doesn't seem to be reaching his lungs.

"I'm only joking!" I holler. Samy goes from an off-shade of vanilla to pinky-white again.

"I'll see what can be managed," Wasim says in an important voice, straightening his back with pride. "Maybe you should practice with me for a while."

"What about the coach?"

"We can play and then I'll approach him about you."

"What's he like?"

"I'm his favorite. So I'm sure he'll listen to my opinion. I'm the goalie and I'm *momtaz*! The coach says so himself."

"I thought you said he was *Englizee*?" Samy says. "How is he calling you *momtaz* when he is a tea-drinking *Englizee*?" Samy crosses his arms over his chest and frowns suspiciously at Wasim.

Wasim is unperturbed. "They learn these words quickly, *ya zalami*. Ali, who is another member of the team, has taught the coach the word *homaar*."

"Why would you have a donkey on a team that is going to Italy?" I ask, crossing my arms over my chest too.

Wasim hits his forehead impatiently. "Oof! You're both sending me to an early grave with your questions. We can't all be *momtaz* all the time. Naturally there will be donkey moves now and then. The point is, I will have some influence with the coach to persuade him to let Samy join."

Samy uncrosses his arms and jumps in the air. "I'm going to Italy!"

"Influence because I am *momtaz*," Wasim adds as an afterthought.

"But you're so short," I say.

"I may look small but I'm fast. That's right, *ya zalami*, I'm fast."

"I'm not a *zalami*."

"*Ya sitti*."

"I'm not your grandmother."

"*Ya oghti*."

"I'm not your sister."

"You're my sister in spirit and I will develop a kidney stone if you don't let me finish!"

"Finish, then, *ya zalami*."

He pauses and looks me in the eye, trying to decide what to make of my comment. Then he grins. "These legs are light and can run circles around the goal! I hear you. You think I'm too tiny to stop the ball. You think I'm exaggerating."

I nod and he waves me silent.

"But trust me, I'm one of our team's best players. The coach is fascinated by my skill. He asked me whether soccer runs in the family. I told him that I'm the first and he thinks I'm gifted. So I'll have a word with him and tell him all about you, Samy. But we must play regularly."

Samy beams.

"I'm hungry," I say as we pass a row of shops and our noses are overcome with the mixed aromas of spicy meat, chicken, and falafels. It's now about nine in the morning and we've only been out of the house for an hour but I already feel as though I've walked to Jordan, never mind the center of Bethlehem.

"Me too," Samy says.

"I'm very hungry," Wasim says. "I played this morning before I went out to work."

"Enough with the soccer!" I yell, throwing my hands in the air.

Samy places an arm around Wasim's shoulders and grins. "She's just jealous."

"So quick to betray your only friend!" I snap and pinch Samy on the arm, making him yelp.

I open my Shrek backpack and take out some fruit and sandwiches of rolled-up Arabic bread with *labne*. "I made extra food in case we have to take the back roads. But we mustn't eat it all or we will have nothing left for later in the day."

"Save your sandwiches," Wasim says. "Let me buy some chips from that shop over there."

"With what?" I instantly feel ashamed and slap my hand over my mouth.

"The money you gave me for the tissues."

"No, keep that. It's yours."

Wasim shakes his head in protest. "This is just for pocket money," he says proudly. "I don't need this money."

He must see the skeptical look in our eyes because he's anxious to reassure us that he's only selling tissues so he can save up for spending money in Italy.

"I want to come back with presents for my family. Do you know they have a building that tips over *and* it's a famous monument?"

"It tips over?" I find that hard to believe. "In *Europe*?"

"Yes! Leans over and people take photos of it and think it's special! Why don't they come to Aida? All our buildings are crooked."

He runs off to the shop to get us bags of chips. We share three flavors and I suddenly feel excited about the empty hummus jar in my bag.

Wasim knows how to get to Jerusalem because his father is an illegal worker there and tries to enter every day without being caught. So Wasim is able to map out the way for us. By the time he's finished, I feel the first rush of doubt flood through me. Maybe I'm being naive to think we could do this. It's not a straightforward trip. It could take a couple of hours or the entire day. We have to take on the checkpoints.

We have to enter Jerusalem without a permit — people get thrown into jail for doing that. And if for some reason we're caught but don't go to jail, there's always the huge fine, which Mama and Baba would find difficult to pay. Not to mention that Sitti Zeynab's village is in West Jerusalem, the "Israeli" side. How will we find her village? Is it still there? Can we move freely without getting caught? I feel sick to my stomach.

"You see," Wasim explains, "the ordinary way to go from Bethlehem to Jerusalem is to first go to Beit Jala, then direct to Jerusalem. This way should only take about fifteen to twenty minutes, depending on what sort of identity card you're registered under. If your parents have a blue identity card, you're a Jerusalemite and can go this way. If they have a green identity card, you're a West Banker. I'm willing to bet my position on the soccer team that you're both green like me!"

We nod solemnly.

"Well, you're *majaneen*. Crazy." Wasim shrugs. "But that's no obstacle. So it's forbidden for you to go the Beit Jala way. You'll have to go another way. But it's full of risk and danger and, of course, much longer. First of all, you have to go from Bethlehem to Beit Sahour, then to Deir Salah, and then to al-Ubaydiyya."

"Oof!" I exclaim. "How long will that take?"

"Bethlehem to Beit Sahour is twenty minutes on foot and five, hmm, maybe six minutes by car. Beit Sahour to Deir Salah is a forty-minute journey on foot and about ten minutes by car. It will take about ten minutes by foot or two minutes by car from Deir Salah to al-Ubaydiyya — one of you should add these figures together — and then after that, you have to pass the Valley —"

"Wadi al-Nar," Samy interrupts, pleased to be able to contribute.

Valley of Fire.

"Wadi al-Nar?" I repeat in a horrified tone.

They both nod.

"I hate it," I say. We drove through the winding and crooked road, full of rocks and sand, on our way to Ramallah some months ago.

"So what?" Samy says with a shrug. "Everybody does."

"It's the only way, so there's no point in complaining," Wasim says. "If you want to avoid it because of the checkpoints then you'll have to cross the hills and mountains by foot. My father crosses over Sheikh Sa'ed, but it's very hard to do so. The hills are steep and rocky and dangerous.

"My father sleeps in the caves there sometimes with other workers who also can't get the permit to work in Jerusalem. They stay overnight in the mountains so that they can try to enter Jerusalem at dawn without being caught. My father's friend Amo Jamal got shot in the thigh once. The soldiers have special radar. They can spot anything with their technology. Anything!"

"Anything?" Samy is, as usual, skeptical.

Wasim looks offended. "My father and his friends were saying that the radar can distinguish a mouse from a human. So yes, *anything*."

"Can they distinguish a human sitting completely still from a big rock?"

"Yes."

"A pair of jeans folded and hidden under a tree from a sleeping lizard?"

"Yes."

"Could they spot a person in the middle of the night, wearing black —"

"Yes!"

"Wait, I haven't finished! Wearing black, curled into a ball completely still . . . except for the fact that they're wriggling their toes?"

Wasim pauses for a moment. I lean forward, watching him closely. "It depends how big the person's toes are, I suppose," he says thoughtfully. "If the person was small and had tiny toes, then maybe they could stand a chance. But if they were big like my father's then, yes, their toes could easily be detected!"

"Especially if they were hairy," I add, thinking about Baba's toes.

"There are wild animals, too, by the way," says Wasim.

"Of course their toes are hairy," Samy says.

"No, I mean there are wild animals in the mountains and hills. My father and his friends come across them all the time."

"What kind of animals?" I'm horrified.

"Snakes, hyenas, wild dogs, and iguanas."

I don't have a choice. We're taking Wadi al-Nar.

"Anyway, after you pass this valley," Wasim continues, "you go through the villages: al-Sawahreh, then

Abu Dis, and finally al-Ayzariyyah. You'll find a checkpoint before you enter the Old City and a soldier will inspect your papers; because you're from the West Bank you'll never be allowed through. But those are just the details."

"Even if you want to turn back, I'm still going ahead," Samy says to me, jutting his chin out boldly. "Can you imagine what everybody at school will say when we tell them we snuck into Jerusalem? That will teach Khader to think he's too good for us."

"Mmm," I mumble as I think of Sitti Zeynab's face, with all those wrinkles and those bright eyes. I look out at the hills and a memory suddenly pops into my head. It's of the time Sitti Zeynab told me about how she met my grandfather and about her wedding in the hills of Jerusalem.

"I lived with my parents and sister in a village on the top of a hill in Jerusalem," she explained one night after I'd woken from another nightmare. "To reach our house you had to climb a steep stone staircase. There were ninety-six stairs. I know because my sister and I counted them many times. My sister was much older than me but still unmarried. Your grandfather had seen a photograph of her and liked what he saw. But the photo was taken when she was eighteen. And the focus was not very sharp, God bless the cameraman. For my sister was not beautiful. Not like I was. This is not immodesty. Just fact. Every time a suitor came for her my parents told me to stay in my room because when the suitor saw me he forgot my sister. She had an unfortunate large mole on her cheek that sprouted hair so thick you could have used it as rope. Her nose was bulbous, her lips thin, and she had gained weight. But her heart was kind and she made me laugh.

"Your grandfather climbed those stairs with his grandmother on his back, the photograph in his pocket."

"His grandmother was on his back?"

"Yes. She was a small old woman, with a sharp tongue and crooked legs, who wanted to approve of the bride. So he hitched her onto his back and ascended the stone stairs. When he arrived and knocked on the door, he was barely breathing."

"He nearly died?"

"No, I mean he was exhausted. Out of breath. And he said that his grandmother had not stopped complaining the entire way up.

"When they arrived my father opened the door." At this point Sitti Zeynab started to chuckle. "Your grandfather and my father exchanged the usual pleasantries and then your grandfather produced the photograph. My father was excited: a suitor for his eldest daughter! He called her into the living room. When she emerged your grandfather was confused. 'But where is the girl in the photograph?' he asked. 'Here I am!' my sister said. Your grandfather was embarrassed. 'There is no *naseeb*, fate, between us,' he mumbled. My sister shrugged and turned away. Nobody can argue with the *naseeb* excuse. As your grandfather stood up to leave, his grandmother turned to my father and said: 'Well, do you have any others? We might as well have a look, seeing as we've come all this way.'

"My father did not wish to hurt my sister's feelings by calling me into the room. But I had heard all the commotion and entered anyway, curious as to who our visitors were. When I saw your grandfather I was dumbstruck. He was very handsome and shy. Our eyes locked and he turned away, embarrassed, but I knew he was pleased. I was a beauty, Hayaat. My back was straight then, not curved like it is now. I had skin as soft as tissue paper. We were married within six months."

"But what about your sister?"

"She married a man who liked her roundness and enjoyed laughing. He also wore thick glasses so I don't think he really noticed the size of the mole. *Naseeb*, fate. It all works out in the end. The hills of Jerusalem sang for us on our wedding days."

I peer out at the landscape. I want to climb those stone stairs, touch the hills where Sitti Zeynab and her sister danced on their wedding days. I want to tear our papers and identity cards into a million tiny pieces and throw them to the wind so that each piece of me can touch my homeland freely.

I ignore the feeling of dread that sits in the pit of my stomach. I'm going to do this.

NINE

We stand at a taxi and bus stop, waiting with a crowd of people near an ice-cream shop. The only people inside are a group of tourists, with their funny accents and cameras. They're crowded around the counter, and the shopkeeper's sallow complexion brightens as he bustles about taking their orders.

"Hey, Samy," I say. "Look at that tourist's T-shirt. It says, *I've been to Jerusalem*." I snort. "He lives closer to Jerusalem than we do."

"What I would give for one of those T-shirts! We could walk into school with it on when we return! Khader would have a fit."

"Khader this and Khader that. Just forget about him."

"Do you know what he said the other day? He said that my father probably turned himself in to the police because he didn't want to look after me!"

"He did not! What? Just out of the blue?"

Samy gives me a sheepish smile. "Well, I had teased him about his new haircut. He looked like a sissy. Oh, and he flunked the history test. So I teased him about that too."

"Samy!" I say in a scolding tone. "And anyway, I thought *you* flunked that test?"

Samy shrugs. "So what? The difference is I don't care. He does."

I throw my hands in the air and roll my eyes.

We wait to board a service, the shared passenger vans that taxi between the cities, towns, and villages. Samy nudges me in the side and then points to two men who stand in front of a taxi, yelling at each other, their hands and arms waving around as they negotiate for air space. They're arguing about a fare, and I marvel at the intensity of their anger. The whole body of the driver, the man on the right, seems engaged in the argument; the man on the left is gesticulating wildly, but, unlike the driver, looks as though he's stepped out of a magazine. He wears a crisp charcoal suit, black sunglasses with gold frames, polished black shoes, and a gray tie.

"*Ya zalami!*" he is shouting. "I always pay fourteen shekels to get to Ramallah! And now you tell me you want double? What has become of us? Now we are cursed by greed!"

"Are you calling me greedy?" The cabdriver is outraged. "I told you that there are rumors of extra checkpoints today. So there is trouble mixed into the equation now. A man is entitled to a little more for his efforts, don't you think?"

The man in the suit shakes his head violently and raises his eyes to the sky. "*Ya Adra!* Oh Virgin Mary! Take the money, oof!" He thrusts the money into the driver's hands and climbs into the backseat of the cab.

The cabdriver sighs, turning to open the front door. Samy runs up to him and cries out, "Wait!"

"What do you want?"

Wasim and I run up behind Samy.

"What kind of trouble?" Samy asks.

The driver looks at him blankly.

"Trouble," Samy repeats. "You mentioned that there is trouble."

"Can we get to al-Ayzariyyah?" I ask.

The cabdriver stares at us. "What happened to your face?"

I raise my hand to touch it and then look down self-consciously.

"Look who's talking," Samy mutters.

"Eh? You rude boy! Where are your manners?"

I step in front of Samy. "Please, Amo," I say, looking sorrowful, "I've been through so much already. Can we get to al-Ayzariyyah?"

"Abu Azam will be here with his service in ten minutes or so. He can take you. Now leave me, I have to take this man-in-a-pressed-suit before I lose my fare." He looks over at Samy and angrily wags his finger. "*Ya ibn al lisaan*, son-of-a-tongue. If you were my son . . ." Samy stares back in defiance until the man throws his hands in the air and gets into his taxi.

We wait among produce vendors, bakery and coffee stands, unloading merchant trucks, commuters, and shoppers. Arabic pop music blasts from passing traffic and collides with tolling church bells and the sound of the Koran being recited over shop-front stereo systems. Whenever a service taxi arrives we inquire as to the name of the driver. Abu Azam arrives twenty minutes later.

He's a fat man. His belt is hitched below an exploding belly and he has a cigarette tucked behind each ear and one dangling from his mouth. It looks impressive and I make a mental note to advise Mama to keep one behind her ear at home too. "Al-Quds! Al-Quds! Jerusalem! Jerusalem!" he cries, like a greengrocer in the market calling out the specials for the day.

Samy and I make a mad rush to the service. "Take us!" we cry, pulling out our pooled funds. "You can get us to al-Ayzariyyah, yes? You're blue!"

"Yes! Hop in."

We turn to Wasim, who's standing with us at the foot of the service door. "If I come with you, my father will kill me," he says. "So I can't."

I offer him the consolation that he's a *momtaz* soccer player. Although I've taken a liking to this Wasim with the packets of tissue paper, I'm not inclined to convince him to accompany us. The idea of listening to him and Samy talk about soccer for hours makes me shudder.

"And Italy!" Samy adds with excitement. "You're going to be a star and we're going to say we knew you!

Don't forget the paper I gave you. It has all my contact information on it, so please tell your *Englizee* coach about me. Then we can play together on the team and be friends."

Wasim beams.

They make arrangements to meet the next day, and Samy makes Wasim promise to bring the *Englizee* coach. "I'm not going to let you escape. I've committed your address to memory!" Samy says and Wasim looks up at Samy, a mixture of reverence and joy in his eyes.

We say our farewells and board the service.

Seated in the front of the bus are two university-age girls clutching bags filled to the brim with heavy textbooks. They both have long wavy hair tied back into ponytails, their bangs hair-sprayed to the side. They're engrossed in conversation, their heads so close I don't know where one ponytail starts and the other ends.

"He said hello to me and I swear he winked."

"He didn't!"

"Yes, he winked and said hello, and I'm in love, I tell you!"

Samy and I exchange a nauseated grimace. Opposite the girls is a man dressed in a navy blue suit, his brown briefcase open wide on his lap. Propped up against the briefcase is a notepad with scribbled writing covering the page. Next to him is an elderly Bedouin with a box of vegetables (tomatoes and lettuce to be exact). He has no teeth. It's frightening. An old woman sits behind him, a large cross dangling from her fossilized neck. She reminds me of Sitti Zeynab because as we pass her on our way to the backseats she starts croaking a prayer for us and for the children of Palestine. She tells nobody in particular that she's hoping to visit her daughter and grandchildren in Abu Dis. She hasn't been there for a while, she laments, and I can almost feel the tension compressed in her tiny frame as her eyes dart anxiously about the van.

We sit at the back of the service, trying to stay as inconspicuous as possible. We're anxious to leave, but Abu Azam insists on filling the service to capacity before moving. There's one more seat to be filled.

Twenty minutes pass and still no movement. Some of the passengers are growing restless and the man with the briefcase cries out to Abu Azam to get the engine started and the bus moving.

"Not yet!" Abu Azam calls back. "I need one more passenger."

"*Ya zalami!* We have places to be. We don't need delays at your end too. As if we don't already have enough obstacles in our way."

"I'll miss my class," one of the girls complains.

Abu Azam jumps out of his seat, his colossal belly following shortly afterward, and stands in front of the door, puffing away on his cigarette with one hand and caressing the one behind his right ear with his other hand. "Patience is a virtue," he says.

"Patience? I have an experiment to monitor."

Abu Azam shrugs and he continues smoking.

A further ten minutes and the man with the brief-case tires of huffing and puffing. He stands up, collects his belongings, and storms out of the bus. "I'll walk," he says, "and probably beat you to it!"

"God be with you, my brother," Abu Azam says in an infuriatingly calm voice.

The man storms away and Abu Azam snickers.

"Who wants to bet me that we'll catch him on our way?"

"Gambling is the work of the devil," the old woman says, and Abu Azam bursts into a fit of laughter.

"*Ya Sitti*, we are all sinners and God is forgiving."

Eventually, a woman clutching a baby approaches the front of the bus. She hands her fare to Abu Azam, who's more than happy to accept. He heaves himself into the driver's seat, adjusting the tape player. A Nancy Ajram pop song blasts through the speakers and the two girls squeal with delight, singing along with the music. The woman raises her baby up in front of her face and starts to sing to him, her face exploding with happiness as the baby coos and smiles back at her.

"Don't tell me you will now wait for another passenger!" the old man cries wearily.

"I lost one, I need to add one."

"*Ya zalami*, let's get this over with!"

"Let's leave!"

"We have places to go!"

Abu Azam throws his hands in the air in defeat. "Enough! *Yallah*, OK, we will leave."

TEN

We drive through the rugged landscape toward Beit Sahour, nearly mowing down an old man wearing a gray *galabiya* hitched up to expose his knees as he rides a donkey.

"What a close one, eh?" Abu Azam cries out merrily, raising his hand outside the window to apologize to the man, who's shaking his fist in anger.

"Do you think she'll be all right?" I ask Samy.

"Who?"

"Sitti Zeynab," I say with a tinge of exasperation.

"I don't know," he responds unhelpfully.

The woman with the baby turns to us, her eyes squinting as she studies our faces.

"Hmm . . . Aren't you Um Tariq's daughter?" she asks me, managing to look at once severe but also pleased.

My heart jolts and I look at Samy in a panic. "Um . . ." I offer pathetically in response.

"Yes! Yes, I know your face! It was ruined by them!" Her face is animated, overcome with the satisfaction that comes with recognition. "Your mother and I used to volunteer at the Arab Women's Union. Hmm . . . that was . . . that was probably about a year ago. Do you remember me? I'm Amto Amal. What are you doing on this bus? And *who* is that boy with you? Your brother was much younger than you, if I remember correctly."

Her voice has assumed the high-pitched, excitable tone of a gossip. I'm very familiar with this voice. Mama and her friends like to meet over tea and sweets, their voices colliding with one another as they exchange stories and rumors. One time I returned from school and told Mama that I had seen Duniya, the daughter of our *dabka* teacher, holding hands with the son of our science teacher. After quizzing me for more details, Mama scolded me for gossiping. "The Prophet says that to talk behind the backs of others is as bad as eating the flesh of one's dead brother. You wouldn't like to eat Tariq's flesh, would you?"

I told Mama that I certainly wouldn't, but as she regularly ate Khalo Sharif's flesh (especially when our neighbor visited with gossip about the flirtatious butcher, Bilal) and had survived, no harm would probably come to me. A tempest erupted. I could see Baba in the background, quietly chuckling to himself.

Amto Amal's tone of voice is like the siren before the dropping of bombs; I know that we're in trouble. I look down at my lap miserably.

"Where are you both going?" she presses.

"Nowhere." My first foolish instinct is denial. I want to grab my words and shove them back into my mouth.

"Passengers on a service do not go *nowhere*!" she cries shrilly. "Why are you on a service all alone?"

All the passengers are staring at us now, watching the scene unfold. *Do you want cushions and pumpkin seeds?* I feel like crying out to them.

My voice stumbles: "Um . . . er . . . mm." The excuse doesn't emerge. I feel tears brimming.

"You're going to make her cry, *ya Sitti*," the old Bedouin man says in a weary tone. "Leave them be." He leans over and offers me a tomato.

"Pah! What's she going to do with a tomato, *ya Haji?*" the old woman with the cross says. "The woman has a point. They are children alone on a bus through Wadi al-Nar."

"Why are you alone?" Amto Amal repeats sternly. "I know this girl's mother," she tells the others. "If she has any idea, she will be sick with fear."

"It's our business," Samy mumbles into his collar.

"Eh? What did you say? Didn't your parents teach you any manners?"

"They taught me to mind my own business," Samy mutters.

Amto Amal stands up and then sits down again. Her mouth gapes open, her eyes bulge with fury. "Never in my life has a boy spoken to me in this way!" She reaches into her handbag and retrieves a cell phone. She scrolls through her address book. "It must be here," she keeps mumbling to herself. "I'm sure it's here."

Samy and I look at each other in a panic. Suddenly the bus swerves to the side of the road and Abu Azam slams his foot on the brake.

"What did I tell you?" he cries. "Oh no! If only we'd put money on my bet."

"Betting is a sin," the old woman says to nobody in particular.

"So is speaking back to an adult!" Amto Amal cries as she fumbles with her phone.

We all look out the windows and see the man in the navy suit sitting on his briefcase on the side of the road. His elbows are leaning on his thighs and his face is cupped in his hands. He looks up at us and grins sheepishly.

Samy and I need no words. The braking is our cue. As the doors open to let the man in, I bolt out, Samy on my heels. We run for the olive groves.

"Don't let them go!" Amto Amal cries.

I look over my shoulder and see her frantically trying to exit the bus, bumping into the man with the briefcase, who looks at her with an expression of confusion. The Bedouin has his head out of the window and is watching us and laughing.

I turn away and we keep on running, my chest bursting with pain as we crash through an avenue of fruit trees and then into the olive groves, dodging over-hanging vegetation and prickly branches. When we know that we've lost them and are far from the view of the road, we stop, throwing ourselves onto the ground on our backs. Every second of every day I take breathing for granted — until now. That steady rhythm of inhaling and exhaling has never felt so sweet.

When at last our bodies have recovered, we stand up and burst into hysterics, clutching on to the sides of our stomachs.

When the fever of laughter has passed, our eyes scan the horizon: olive groves flanked by hills and rolling mountains. A herd of goats and sheep are grazing at a near distance. A pang of love for my country suddenly strikes through me. The lazy way the trees and bushes dot the land. The effortless beauty of the mountains and the secrets hidden within them.

But then the ubiquitous Wall, twisting and turning, devouring the landscape, towering over the fields, villages, and towns.

"So where are we now?" I ask Samy, walking over to a tree and leaning on its trunk. The trunks of the olive trees are like thick wrists, some more slender and feminine than others. Their branches caress the ground like somebody drumming their fingers on a table.

We establish that we've passed Beit Sahour and are probably in between it and Deir Salah, which, according to Wasim's advice, is about a forty-minute walk. We decide that the most logical plan is to return to the road and keep following it until we reach Deir Salah, where we'll catch a service. We're confident that we'll bump into Deir Salah along the road.

It feels so strange to walk rather than drive down a main road. In the bus, I stared out at the dusty surface, one long, mundane stretch. On foot, the road has character: stones, rocks, twigs, potholes, tire tracks. Our shoes blacken within moments. Each car and bus that zooms past us throws up a cloud of dust that tickles our eyes and makes us sneeze.

The stones and rocks fascinate me. Maybe it's because we're tired and bored. I pick up the interesting ones and give them names. The one with the smooth surface and oblong shape is Abu Yasser. Somehow it reminds me of his bald, long head. The rough one with the oddly shaped clefts and crevices is Samer, the boy in the year above us at school who picks his pimples and has holes all over his face.

I'm examining another stone when Samy says unexpectedly: "It will be seven years exactly in two weeks."

I hesitate. "How long has it been since you saw him?"

"Three years."

"Why so long?"

"We're not allowed to visit anymore."

"Do you write?"

"Sometimes."

I wait for him to continue and when he doesn't I say: "You should send photos."

"We do. Amto Christina sends them. But I would rather he didn't get them."

"Why? It would be nice for him. He can stick them on the wall next to his bed."

"She insists on me posing in trousers and a shirt with my hair combed like a sissy. I can just imagine what the other prisoners must say to him."

"Does he write back?"

"Sometimes. It can be annoying, though."

"Why?"

"Well, I usually receive his letters late, so by the time I read them they're outdated and I've already sent him several more letters in the meantime. He sent me a letter at Easter last year. But by the time I received it, months had gone by, including my birthday. Of course the birthday card was months late too."

"Oh, I see what you mean."

We walk on in silence for a few moments until I say: "Samy, your father's a hero. Locked up all these years for no reason other than organizing protests and strikes."

He cuts me off swiftly. "He traded me for the cause."

I say something useless in an attempt to comfort him but he ignores me. "Just imagine, Hayaat," he says. "Italy . . . A real soccer team. I'm dizzy thinking about it."

ELEVEN

We finally reach the village of Deir Salah. We wait at the bus stand, leaning on the wall of a nearby house, enjoying the shade of an apricot tree. A small crowd of people waits with us.

Samy looks bored and is rubbing his hand on his cheek.

"Does this look like stubble to you?" he asks me in a hopeful voice.

"More like dust from the road."

The small talk of the crowd is cut by voices coming from the other side of the small, dusty incline that leads to the bus stand. At first the voices are muffled; slowly, as the distance narrows, there's another language in the air. The collective mood of the crowd shifts. Bodies stiffen, ears prickle.

I assume the people speaking Hebrew are soldiers ready with their guns and fatigues to set up a flying checkpoint. The only Israelis we know are the ones who give us orders — who map out our lives every day, controlling where we go, who we see, and when we move.

The older people begin to rummage in their pockets, bags, and wallets, ready to present their identity cards. The resigned looks on their faces terrify me. The *shabab*, the teenagers and twenty-something-year-olds, stand still, their faces defiant. They pretend to look at ease but I can see the tension in their jaws, the stiffness in their backs.

I look over at Samy and for a second I don't recognize him. He has a hardened look in his eyes and the muscles in his neck spring out. In that moment I realize what it means to have a parent alive and yet feel like an orphan. Because while Samy's mother's death couldn't be prevented, his father's life is in the hands of the Israeli army.

A middle-aged man and woman emerge from over the hill. The woman has a mass of brown curls that bobs up and down as she walks. The man's hair is slicked back into a low ponytail, tight black curls jutting out of the elastic band. They don't wear military uniforms. They wear jeans and T-shirts. Instead of guns they hold water bottles. Their voices are loud and energetic. They speak Hebrew, but have a shawl in the colors of the Palestinian and Israeli flags draped over their shoulders. Samy and I stand in awe, watching and waiting for them to make a move.

They approach us, smiling as though it's the most natural scene in the world. Then they greet us in fluent Arabic, introducing themselves as David and Mali. Mali's eyes are crinkled and kind. She smiles easily, her self-confidence obvious in the way she holds her back straight, her neck swanlike. David, on the other hand, seems slightly tense. Tall and lanky with an almost gray face, he has large midnight-blue eyes that have a sheen of desperation. He smiles anxiously, as if longing to be understood, to be trusted. His vulnerability makes me feel powerful. I don't want to let go of this feeling. For an ugly moment, I want David to grovel.

A couple of the younger men and women in the

crowd look at David and Mali curiously, some with suspicion and apprehension.

"What do you mean by wearing that shawl?" one asks. "You're Israelis."

"Yes, but *against* the occupation," David says and laughs nervously.

Ahh. Heads nod in acknowledgment. It's not unusual for us to meet international as well as Israeli peace activists visiting the West Bank, offering their solidarity by planting olive trees, staging vigils at checkpoints or at the Wall, mediating with settlers on behalf of people who are prevented from accessing their land.

"We're peace activists," Mali says, "on our way to Jerusalem."

"So why don't you take the Israeli-only bypass road?" I exclaim. "It's much quicker. It's direct!" I feel as though I'm revealing a wonderful truth to them. Maybe they don't know that as Israelis they can easily travel to Jerusalem.

"We're on checkpoint watch," Mali says.

Samy and I look at each other and back at them, clearly indicating that we think they're crazy.

The service minivan destined for Jerusalem via Wadi al-Nar arrives moments later, and Samy and I cheer.

"Ahlan, welcome to the service!" Samy sings, twirling and dancing in the spot. "God bless the service!"

He grabs my hand and we dance the *dabka,* twirling a tissue in the air as we kick and step around our audience. Some of the people laugh.

We pay for our tickets and board, taking our seats at the rear. The service is typically run-down, with the seats almost reduced to springs, the left-hand mirror absent, and the driver's ashtray overflowing. A large vanity mirror like the one Mama uses to pluck her eyebrows is duct-taped into the empty frame of what was once a rearview mirror. Photographs of three grinning children and a stern-looking elderly man wearing traditional Palestinian dress are stuck on the dashboard.

Mali and David climb onboard and sit on the seats in front of us. David is so tall he has to hunch over as he enters to avoid a nasty bump from the low door. Passengers slowly fill up the service until we're a total of eight. Everybody introduces themselves, *assalamu alaikoms* ringing through the air.

"I must first check the water and play with the motor a little," the bus driver tells us. "Here, listen to some music while you wait."

He turns on the stereo system and Kazem al-Saher blasts through the speakers. Samy and I turn our noses up in frustration.

"He sings classical poetry!" I moan.

"Put some pop music on!" Samy cries.

The bus driver raises the volume and grins. "Pop music? Huh!"

Through the open windows, I can hear the driver singing out of tune as he fiddles with the engine, oblivious to the pain he's causing us.

"We have Israelis with us on the bus," I whisper to Samy as softly as I can. "That means we can probably get through the checkpoints."

"They're probably agents," he hisses into my ear. "Like the ones who took my father."

I lean my elbow on my thigh, cup my chin in my hand, and study David's face: his *Israeli* face. The eyelids, the nose, the mouth: so ordinary. The rough stubble around the pointy chin: It could have been the stubble that Baba grew in between breakfast and lunch. Put David in the olive fields, in a pew in the Church of Nativity, in the bazaar at Manger Square, in a *keffiyeh*, in a *galabiya*, and nobody would know the difference between him and a Christian or a Muslim.

"The Jews and Arabs are cousins," my teacher told us. "We descend from Prophet Abraham." But I've never been sure what to do with this piece of information.

"Where do you come from?" a woman who introduces herself as Grace asks them.

"We were both born in Tel Aviv," Mali replies in Arabic. "But we're now dual citizens of both the United States and Israel. We're back for a visit. We're working with a human rights watch group."

"But you both speak Arabic very well," a young woman called Nirvine remarks.

"We've studied Arabic," David says.

"They have television accents," Samy whispers in my ear as David explains where they've studied and the Arab countries they've visited. "We're Arabs. We know phlegm when we hear it. It's probably part of the training. The American accent is a cover."

"They don't look like agents," I whisper back. "She's

wearing red nail polish on her toes and he has a pierced eyebrow." I tap my finger against my forehead. "Do you think it would hurt?"

"Even if it did, they're probably used to pain. Part of the training. An earring in the eyebrow is nothing to him."

One of the men on the service introduces himself as Raghib. He's wearing a thick pair of glasses and his eyes appear as tiny brown dots. Like Samy's uncle Joseph, he's combed the few strands of hair on his head to the side, but the exposed parts of his balding head are shiny. He looks funny, but when he speaks, his voice is gentle.

"And how is it possible that Israelis can sit here with us, wrapped in the flags of two people?" he asks.

"We're peace activists," Mali explains.

"Ahh! Hippies!" Nirvine says through giggles.

David raises his eyebrows and smiles. "Not quite."

"So what's your story, then?" Grace asks. "Sorry to pry, but the majority of Israelis I encounter have guns in their hands."

"Well," David says, running his fingers through his hair, "we're here because we report back about the human rights abuses. We don't all support what's happening."

"Yes, we know that," Nirvine murmurs, while several other people clear their throats.

Samy nudges me in the side. "Do you think he's lying?"

I shrug, still trying to make up my mind.

"We want a just peace," David says.

Mali interrupts. "We're here because we care about justice for everyone."

"Don't tell us," Grace says. "Go tell your government."

"You want me to prove my worth?" David says a little testily. "I've paid a price for my beliefs. That's why I live in America now. I was forced to leave my birthplace. I'm a *refusenik*. I was part of the IDF —"

"You were part of the army?" I'm shocked.

All eyes are now boring holes into David.

"You were part of the army?"

"The IDF?"

"You were part of the occupation?"

David sits upright in his chair. "Yes, conscription is compulsory. I was eighteen and had to enlist."

"David, you were part of the army?"

"David, are we terrorists?"

Raghib roars at us to be quiet. "Let him finish!" he hollers. "Let him tell his story."

"Yes, let him finish."

"We're being rude."

"Let him talk."

"Let us be quiet and let David speak."

David fidgets in his seat. "And I thought Jews were the only people who spoke over each other," he says softly.

For a moment there's blank silence and then, as glances are exchanged among the passengers, an eruption of laughter. Something in the air changes.

"Yes, I was part of the IDF," he continues, his voice relaxing. "I grew up believing in a land without a people for a people without a land. Don't mistake me. I believe in Israel. That may offend you, but it's who I am. But I'm against what's happening. I just want to do what I can in my own way."

"You believe in one people taking over the land of another people?" Grace asks.

David runs his fingers through his hair. "Look, it's

complicated, I know. I don't have all the answers. I just want the occupation to end, and then we can talk about how to sort this mess out."

Nirvine smiles at him. "Well, it's good to have people like you supporting us."

"They have fallen for him, naive fools," Samy whispers to me. I tell him to shut up as I want to hear what David has to say.

"When I was in Gaza, we took over a Palestinian home that was in a strategic position. The family had no choice in the matter. We arrived and forced our way in. We ordered the family to live on the bottom floor, a family of nine in one living room. We took the second level and the rooftop. Some of the soldiers trashed the rooms. They thought it was fun to write on the walls and mirrors and ransack the family's belongings. It sickened me when I saw they had written *Gas the Arabs* on one of the walls."

"I've seen that," Nirvine says quietly. "On a wall in Hebron."

"When the family wanted to use the toilet, they had to ask our permission," David continues, "as the toilet was on the second floor. One day, the father needed to use the bathroom. Some of the other soldiers teased and taunted him. They made him wait." He takes a deep breath and shakes his head. "I watched as the inevitable happened. The man broke, and the wet patch spread right before the eyes of his children. But it is his eyes that will haunt me forever. . . . That night I refused to serve for a minute longer. I was imprisoned, eventually tried, and sentenced to a term of seven months. After I was released, I left for America. I settled down and eventually became a dual citizen."

My skin prickles. I imagine strange men in my home, strapped with machine guns, sleeping in my bed, smoking on my rooftop, telling me when I can use my bathroom. I try to picture David in his army fatigues. But I can't. I'm momentarily overcome with mixed emotions. It's less complicated to think of all Israelis as my oppressors. It's less complicated to resent them all.

"I don't envy your soldiers their power for one moment." These words are spoken by a middle-aged man sitting in front of David and Mali. He introduces himself as Marwan. He has earphones dangling down his chest, the faintest sound of rock music streaming out. He wears jeans, a striped pastel blue shirt, and a gold chain. His shoes fascinate me: scaly gray leather, and so pointed at the front I think he might be able to reach the dashboard with the slightest flick of his foot. Propped up against the window beside him is a large *oud* case. "You know something?" he says. "I'm afraid for the future of your children just as much as I'm afraid for the future of mine."

Grace shifts in her seat, fanning herself with her handbag. "I don't pity them," she says. "I see the way they look at us at the checkpoints and roadblocks, like animals to be herded. Why should I pity them, *ya* Marwan? I am sorry, David and Mali, but there is no room in my heart anymore to care for those who sit on the stolen tops of our mountains, watching us as though we're insignificant cockroaches."

"And that is why," Marwan says, "the occupation steals from the humanity of the occupier *and* the occupied. We are all losers."

Grace purses her lips and then, her voice taut, says: "Perhaps. But I did not ask for my land to be occupied, and to be honest I don't care about my attitude when I find it difficult to feed my children and give them a safe future. It will never end, I tell you. Sometimes I feel I have given up hoping."

"The grown-ups have gone mad," Samy mutters.

"Shall we solve the Middle East peace process here?" Raghib says with a gentle smile.

Grace looks down at her hands and then sighs. "I'm sorry, David and Mali. I didn't mean anything against you both personally."

Mali raises her hand, motioning for Grace to stop apologizing. "We understand how you feel."

"They're decent," I whisper to Samy.

"They train them to lie, silly."

I roll my eyes at him.

"Well," Raghib interrupts, "I can tell you now that the Middle East conflict will erupt if that driver does not hurry up. What's happening, *ya zalami?*" Raghib leans out of the window. "It has been fifteen minutes now!"

The bus driver stands up, dusts his trousers, and jumps into his seat, slamming the door behind him. "If I could only get my hands on that stupid mechanic in Beit Sahour! I am sorry, my friends. Oof! *Yallah! La ilaha ilalah!*" He squirms in his seat, trying to get into a comfortable position. He lights a cigarette and then turns to face us, the smoke curling its way out of his mouth to hang thick in the stale, hot air. "We have guests with us today. I am Karim, and I extend a warm welcome to our friends Mali and David. Ignore these people who are interrogating you. I don't care if you pray in a synagogue or shave your hair for Buddha. Anybody who wants peace and pays their fare is welcome on my service. Sorry there is no air-conditioning. It broke down sometime in the seventies. Huh! God knows why you wish to travel through Wadi al-Nar. Maybe my bus is so very charming that you can't resist the ripped seats, yes?"

The driver's good humor is infectious, and Mali and David smile.

"You are both crazy, huh? Good! We need more crazy people in this land. It is just the thing we are lacking! Huh! If the bus crashes over the side of the mountain, the authorities will scratch their heads. Jewish, Muslim, Christian bodies! Huh! What fun it would be to see their faces!"

TWELVE

The bus jerks its way along the road that leads us past the village of al-Ubaydiyya on our way to the Valley of Hell. For a moment I'm sure we're going to die as Karim uses his knees to maneuver the steering wheel while he pours tea from a battered-looking red thermos into a plastic cup. "Would anybody like some?" he says, raising the thermos in the air.

"Put your hands on that steering wheel!" Nirvine shrieks.

"Yes, yes, *ya* madam," he says. "Do not fear. These roads are my home. I can drive this bus blindfolded. In fact, I have. Let me tell you a story. . . ."

I shut out his voice and lean my head against the heated aluminum window frame, desperate for a gust of cool wind to blast over my face. A metallic taste sets in my mouth, and the pit of my stomach churns as the bus winds its way through the massive valley, negotiating the narrow unpaved lanes that I'm sure were intended for donkey carts, not cars and minivans. In some sections of the road there's no fencing or railing between the road and the edges of the mountains. Nothing to protect us from dropping to our deaths, particularly with a driver who seems to think there's nothing wrong with drinking *chai*, smoking a cigarette, and handling a steering wheel all at the same time. With every skid and bump, I watch Grace frantically cross her heart and mutter a prayer. David and Mali are bent over clipboards writing notes. Marwan clutches on to his *oud* case as he leans his head against the windowsill. Nirvine sits in the front seat listening to Karim's story, interjecting with a "Watch out!" and "Slow down!" every now and then. Raghib's head is snapped backward against the seat, his Adam's apple bobbing up and down as he gently snores.

Instead of a cool breeze, harsh specks of dust fly into my face as we drive over the snaking dirt track. I rub my eyes, feeling uneasy. It's noon and I'm expected home from school by four. I wonder whether Mama and Baba are at Sitti Zeynab's bedside.

I stare out the window. Parts of the landscape are rugged, rocky, and sparse. The colors of the hills melt into one another, gold into brown into cream into beige, leaving me unable to tell where one hill starts and another one ends.

We trek down a steep incline, and I hold on to my seat tightly and take deep breaths, concentrating on my lungs, on pushing the air in and out, even as I feel the wheels of the bus slide against the dusty road. A trail of sweat oozes down my legs, a couple of beads dripping into my thick white socks. I remember Maysaa and me at our first *dabka* practice, how we competed for the teacher's attention. I resented her that first time, with her coordination and nimble feet. And then we became the best of friends. . . . I touch my face, tracing the scars. The memories flood through me, and I rap my knuckles on my forehead to dislodge them. Then I lean my head against the back of the seat in front of me and close my eyes, trying to distract myself with happy memories. I think of Sitti Zeynab. The memory of her always warms me.

It was only a couple of months ago when I sat beside her, wearing a pink pastel dress, lined with tulle and beaded around the collar with itchy sequins. I was sitting like a ruffled doll in our living room as Jihan's future in-laws spoke with my parents about the wedding plans and ate syrupy *knafa* and smoked their Winston Blues. Sitti Zeynab sat quietly beside me, listening to the adults talk but not bothering to make a contribution. Ahmad sat like a starched shirt, respectfully averting his eyes from Jihan, who raised her teacup to her lips but avoided actually sipping so as not to ruin her lipstick. The adults started to argue about the best wedding hall.

"But Abu Sofyan's hall has the smoke machine," Ahmad's mother said.

"What do you mean, a smoke machine?" Baba asked. "Everybody can buy their cigarettes before the wedding."

"Not cigarettes," Mama said. "The machine they use when the couple slow dances."

"It has a nice effect."

"I don't like the smell."

"What about Joe's Palace? They have chicken, meat, *and* prawns."

"I don't like the color scheme. Too much pink."

Sitti Zeynab leaned close to me and whispered, "In the old days all you needed for a good wedding was music, food, and a star-filled night. Let's send the lot of them up to the rooftop and throw the wedding party there. Less headache."

I grinned. The pink tulle scratched my legs. My hair, pulled up high, felt heavy and tight.

"I want to let my hair down, it's itchy," I told Sitti Zeynab.

"Let it down, *habibti*. They won't notice anyway, they're too busy discussing whether the smoke machine is run on gas or electricity."

But nothing could escape Mama's sharp ears and, through gritted teeth, she hissed: "What would Ahmad's parents think?"

And so I sat in that wretched living room, and I scratched my legs and poked at my hair so that Ahmad's parents would not think.

"Pah!" Sitti Zeynab muttered, rolling her eyes at Mama. "Think? I'll give them some gas to think about in a minute." She winked at me and I giggled.

Suddenly, Karim utters a curse. His voice shatters through my thoughts. The service slows down.

"Sorry, my friends," he says, shaking his head in frustration. "They have put a flying checkpoint along the way today."

A couple of military jeeps are blocking the road with some makeshift concertina wire set up. Flanking both sides of the jeep are soldiers, each strapped with an M-16. They wear black sunglasses and hold walkie-talkies. An urge to urinate hits me with a jolt, and I squeeze one leg over the other.

A large number of cars and service vans are parked in single file along the edge of the narrow valley road. Most of the vehicles are empty, the passengers and drivers standing outside, rummaging through their bags and wallets, ready to produce their identity cards. I try to divert my eyes from the soldiers' guns as my bladder swells impatiently, demanding my attention. *Shut up!* I scream in my head. *I don't have time for you now!*

"I mean, really," Karim says with a sigh, "with drivers hardly ever able to reach even fourth gear thanks to these checkpoints, they're doing us a favor. Saving us gas, you know. Well, let us hope David and Mali are our saving grace."

"Karim, we're Israelis *against* the occupation," David says. "We don't expect any sympathy from the soldiers."

"But we have our cameras," Mali says. Noticing our open mouths, she continues. "The Internet is your most powerful weapon."

"Great," Nirvine says with a chuckle, "we'll be famous all over the world. Should I apply more lipstick?"

One of the soldiers approaches the service van and leans in the doorway, a stern expression on his face. "Get out of the van," he says in broken Arabic. "Pass ready."

"Donkey," I hear somebody, perhaps Raghib, mutter. "At least learn how to get the plural imperative right."

I steal a questioning glance at Samy, but he shrugs his shoulders. *Majnoon*, he discreetly mouths to me. *Crazy.*

We all climb out of the service van and lean against it, watching the interaction of the soldiers with the line of people in front of us. Families, men and women in workers' uniforms, old people in traditional dress, children our age and younger who look as restless as I feel.

Directly ahead of us is a woman who stands before one of the soldiers, her two children clutching on to her long gray skirt. She's arguing, her voice rising with frustration. If she looked down she would see one of her children, a girl of about seven, tapping the boy, about six years old, on the arm. He quickly returns the tap. She taps again. He scowls, reaches out, and pinches her. It's a pinch with a twist, the ones Mama reserves for Tariq and me when we've broken something or embarrassed her in front of guests and she's feeling particularly sadistic. The girl howls and the mother finally looks down at her children and yells at them to shut up, adjusting her bag on her shoulder as she tries to regain her composure. The girl tries to explain that her brother has broken the rules and met a tap with a pinch, but the mother, like Mama, is not interested in the causes, just the effects. She yanks her children's arms close to her side and gives them the silencing look that Jihan informs me all mothers are trained in during prenatal classes. The mother then looks back at the soldier, who, and I swear to God this is true, looks, for a second, like he's trying to suppress a smile. Then he sneezes and I wonder if I've misread a facial twitch.

Samy stands beside me, digging a hole in the ground with his heel.

"What are you thinking about?" I whisper.

"Soccer. Do you think Amo Joseph will let me go to Italy? If the coach accepts me into the team? The coach will, you know. Wasim is much smaller than me. I can't see why he wouldn't, with my defense skills. If I get the coach to tell Amo Joseph I'm going to visit the Vatican, he has to let me play! I will never forgive him if he forbids me from joining the team. Forget his and Amto Christina's obsession with hell! They're so intent on rescuing me from God's hell that they can't see I want to be rescued from this. I hate them!"

"Samy!"

His eyes squint in fury.

"Don't say that," I continue. "They've looked after you since —"

"Don't give me your pity! And don't ask me to shut my mouth because Baba sits in prison! It's his fault I'm alone with these Jesus-this and Jesus-that bores."

"Samy! He was working against the occupation. He's a hero!"

"Working against the occupation is stupid. There's no point. The reward is death or imprisonment. He didn't care about me. He didn't care about how it would affect me if I lost him. Stuff him and everybody."

I don't know how to respond. I know Samy's temper well. The constant fights at school, the talking back to adults, the tantrums during soccer games, the disappearing acts he pulls on us all after an argument with his uncle and aunt. "Your temper is too old for you!" Ostaz Ihab scolded Samy once. "It sits on you like an adult's clothes. Change your attitude, *ya* Samy!"

The soldier is shaking his head and the woman turns on her heel, her children exchanging angry words at each other as she pulls them to a taxi. She opens her purse and gives some money to the taxi driver standing outside the vehicle. She reaches into the open rear window and retrieves a couple of bags and a small potted plant. She takes a second look at the potted plant and then, a look of irritation on her face, tosses it onto the ground. The children look confused and the girl reaches down to grab it.

"Leave it," the mother orders. "*Yallah*, we're walking."

"But I don't want to walk," the boy whines. The mother rolls her eyes and sighs and they start down the meandering road on foot.

The line is long. The soldiers search cars and bags and scan their eyes over identity cards. Some people are allowed to drive on. Some are ordered to walk. Some cars are turned away. Some bags are emptied completely. Others are given a cursory glance. There seems no system in place. No consistency. The rules are as unpredictable as the soldiers' moods.

There's a cloud of humiliation looming over us as the soldiers scold women when they don't empty their bags quickly enough and order some of the men to remove their shirts and raise their arms in the air.

Samy nudges me in the side and says: "Look at that guy's gut. How much *mansaf* do you think he eats in a week? He probably hasn't seen his knees in years."

"I suppose the soldiers have a right to check him. He could easily hide some dynamite in his layers of fat."

He laughs and the man in front of us abruptly turns to face us.

"This is not a joke," he says.

I look down at my feet, shamefaced. Samy stares boldly back at him and, in as melodramatic a voice as he can muster, says: "We haven't laughed in weeks."

The man's frown smooths out. "Well, I haven't laughed in years."

"House demolished? Family member imprisoned? Killed?"

"Some of this. And some of that," he says matter-of-factly. "But mainly, it's because of my mother-in-law."

Samy and I trade blank looks. "She's part of the IDF?"

"No, she's a terrorist organization of her own making. I can't even have a cup of coffee in peace."

When our turn eventually arrives, my bladder has surprisingly resorted to gently throbbing rather than betraying me. It has finally learned the meaning of loyalty and is, thankfully, behaving itself.

"What will we do?" I ask Samy in a panic. "Where will we say we're going?"

"Abu Dis?" Samy suggests in a low voice.

"Yes, visiting family, if he asks."

"Passes?" one of the soldiers demands in broken Arabic. His uniform is crisp and olive green. His army fatigues are tight at the thighs and then bunch up around his calves, straightening down at his ankles. I can imagine him getting ready for work in the morning: ironing his uniform, polishing his big black boots, cleaning the frames of his glasses with a special cloth. I'm suddenly interested in him. What does he do after a hard day's work in the occupied territories? Does he have a home to go to or does he live with the army? How old is he? Maybe he's married with kids. I imagine him at home with his family in the evening, all of them gathered around the oblong dinner table. There would be a wife and her name would be Esther, and two, no, three children: Sarah, Aaron, and Ehud. They would be eating and watching an episode of Israeli *X Factor*, if there is such a thing, until their father demands they switch it off at dinnertime.

I look at the soldier as he studies Samy's birth certificate. He's not very old but his face is tough, like leather.

As he turns to me and asks for my papers, fear replaces my curiosity. I can sense him staring at my scars. My instinct is to touch my face. My shaking hands reach out, as if to hide my shame. They fumble over my scar, and my birth certificate slips out of my sweaty palms and drops on the ground. The butt of his gun jiggles as he bounces impatiently on the spot.

I'm in danger of falling back into the dark pool of my memories; the sound of bullets whistling past my ears is so real. Samy steps down hard on my foot. I jump and the soldier studies me, a bewildered look on his face.

"So nervous and jittery," he says somewhat half-heartedly in Arabic. "Why are you acting like you have something to hide?"

It's all I can do to stop myself from wetting my pants. "Nothing . . . nothing to hide."

I crouch down and pick up my birth certificate. I hand it to him. He glances at it, returns it to me, and then points his gun at me, using its butt to motion for me to step aside.

David and Mali step forward. They speak in Hebrew, their voices rising and falling. The soldier frowns and then, after an excruciating moment of silence, he walks back to his comrades and busies himself on the phone.

Five, ten, fifteen minutes pass until the soldier returns. I've bitten down into my nails, peeling at the cuticles with my teeth. Samy sits on the side of the road, his face grim and tense as he watches the soldiers' every move. Karim, Grace, Nirvine, Marwan, and Raghib stand patiently; their faces seem calm. The sun blazes over us and, not for the first time that day, I wish I were sitting in an icy cold bath.

The soldier returns and says something to David and Mali. David yells something back and the soldier shakes his head. Mali gives the soldier a look of disgust. The soldier shrugs, turns, and walks back to the line to search through another car.

"We have to walk," David and Mali say apologetically.

"To where?" Samy cries.

"The Container checkpoint."

"That makes no sense!" Grace says.

"What does sense have to do with it?" Raghib moans.

"We're sorry," Mali says. "We tried."

"It's not your fault," Grace says quietly.

"No, it's not your fault," Nirvine repeats.

"Karim, I'm sorry, my friend," Mali says. "But you have to return to Bethlehem. You aren't allowed through."

Karim mutters a curse under his breath and then shrugs, pops a cigarette out of his pocket, and lights it with a match before he speaks. He flicks the match onto the ground.

"What's the problem?" Marwan asks.

"Like I know," David says. "The soldier tried to get us through, but his commander says no. They must have run my name through the system. A *refusenik* is obviously not a welcome hero. Lucky for my American passport or there'd be some serious trouble."

"There's that word again," I whisper to Samy. "What's a *refusenik*?" He shrugs as if to say, How would I know?

"So why are some vehicles allowed through while others are being turned back?" I ask.

"Who knows?" David says wearily. "Maybe they don't like Karim's face here." His joke is forced, but Karim plays along.

"My good looks are a security threat. I tell my wife that all the time but she doesn't believe me."

"So we *walk*?" Nirvine cries. "How much more can I take of this?" She beats her chest with her hand and cries out to the sky, "God give me patience!"

"It's OK," Karim says gently. "Walk on and catch one of the service vans that are allowed to pass."

"And then what?" she asks. "We still have the Container checkpoint to pass."

Karim points a finger to the sky. "Trust in God, my sister. There is no other way."

Nirvine shakes her head. "I don't have the energy to walk in *heels*, try to flag down another service, and then calm my nerves as I wait to see if they'll let me pass through the Container. Will they have me wait obediently like a trained dog for their permission to leave one of my own towns and enter another? Not today. No, I'll return with you. My sister will have to wait. She can send me photos of the baby by e-mail."

And so Nirvine turns back with Karim and the rest of us walk past the flying checkpoint, along the valley road. As we start, we pass a family standing at the open trunk of a taxi. A soldier stands over them as they remove boxes of wrapped gifts, three suitcases, and an electric blue tricycle from the trunk. The tricycle has red wheels and yellow handlebars with silver ribbon wrapped around them.

The soldier is yelling at the driver to turn back.

An old woman is with them, tears streaming down her face as her eyes fix on the soldier's gun. The driver's hands are squeezed tight over the steering wheel.

"Don't be afraid," Marwan leans down and whispers in my ear.

But I can't help it. I watch as the man argues with his wife about throwing gifts away, about there being too many to carry. The woman insists, and they distribute the gifts among themselves and their three children, who are clinging to the old woman. The man carries the two larger suitcases, balancing the tricycle on one of them. The children balance boxes of gifts against their chests. The woman holds on to the old woman with one free arm, using her other arm to tuck a suitcase under her armpit. The soldier watches as the family starts walking. The man, woman, children, and old woman stop after several steps to collect their energy. Then, without speaking, they continue, pausing for breath after every few feet. Their faces are twisted with anger and exhaustion.

I try to put them out of my mind as we overtake them. We kick our feet against the dust, pant our way through the sloppy heat, stop to remove stones that have crept into our shoes, and after several miles, wave down a van that has been allowed to pass through. We squeeze ourselves in along the already crowded seats and aisle and then carry on with our journey to the Container checkpoint. As I sit squashed like a chickpea in a hummus jar, I can't help wondering how many hours it will take for that family to battle the road with their suitcases, tarnished gifts, and that sad little tricycle.

THIRTEEN

The service slows down. We approach the end of a long line of cars, taxis, minitrucks, and vans. I notice three Palestinian men crouched down on their knees on the side of the road, their eyes blindfolded, their hands tied behind their backs. Four soldiers stand some thirty feet away, casually chatting among themselves.

"Why is it called Container checkpoint?" I ask Raghib. I'm pressed up against a window, Raghib directly in front of me.

"Because it's shaped like a container."

A man sandwiched beside us interrupts. "No, *ya zalami*, you're wrong. It's because a man who owned a merchandise container set up shop in it to sell cigarettes, chewing gum, soft drinks, *ya'ni* things like this to the travelers who passed through Wadi al-Nar."

"No, no, you are both wrong," a woman calls out in

a shrill voice. "It is because we're all like sardines in a container!" She cackles at her joke and a couple of others join her.

I peer out of the window. Concrete blocks and boulders litter the ground and a large freestanding watchtower is on the right of us. A group of soldiers stands beside a military jeep. The vehicles are lined up thirty to fifty feet away. The soldiers are allowing one car through at a time.

"Can't we get out?" someone calls to the driver.

The heat is stifling, inducing unwelcome body odor. We're a spectrum of ages but all equally irritable. Samy's face is turned up in disgust. I catch a whiff of a fart. Even under occupation people still claim the right to release gas in a crowd. Maybe it's the anonymity of a packed service cab that encourages them. People cough and splutter as the offensive odor reaches their noses. A woman cries out: "For God's sake, ask him if we can get out. I'm ready to faint in here!"

"I'll speak to them," David says.

But the driver has already taken the lead and, poking his head out of the window and motioning to a nearby soldier, calls out, "Can we stretch our legs?"

The soldier looks back at the driver with a bored expression. Without bothering to answer, he turns his head away.

"Was that a yes or a no?" the driver asks, consulting us. "If it was a yes, he would have at least nodded, right? If it was a no and we get out, there'll be trouble. It's safer to just stay in."

"Yes, because he has the most comfortable seat in the van," a woman behind me mutters.

"That's not fair," somebody responds. "You can't expect him to share the driver's seat."

"Who does that soldier think he is?" Mali says indignantly. "Ignoring us like that!"

It's getting unbearably stuffy and claustrophobic. Somebody's bag juts into my back. The summer sun is burning strongly, cooking us in the van like chickens in an oven. We're all getting restless and a man soon cries out: "Cramps! I have cramps in my feet!"

"Push your feet in the other direction," somebody flippantly suggests.

"You are dreaming if you think there's room!" the man snaps back. "Move! Please! I must get out! It's unbearable!"

I feel myself being squeezed even more against the window. The man tries to push his way through and over the passengers. The crush intensifies as people groan and cry out, yelling for the door to be opened as the man moans, "My feet! My feet!"

The driver is forced to activate the handle to open the door as he helplessly cries out a warning: "But he didn't nod!"

We spill out of the van, blindly grabbing on to one another as we struggle to get down the step and make contact with the ground. The man with the cramps falls on the earth, throwing his shoes off and frantically pushing his feet upward.

The din of shouts and cries propels two of the soldiers toward our van. They run forward, holding up their weapons and yelling out orders for us to get back in. One of them points his gun in our direction and I let out a small scream. Raghib grabs me and almost throws me back into the van. "Get back in!" he shouts and the passengers practically jump on top of one another as they try to squeeze back through the door. David and Mali cry out for everybody to calm down, yelling out to the soldiers in Hebrew.

I look around for Samy. With the exception of the man with the cramps and David and Mali, he's the last to enter. His movements are slow and controlled. He climbs the step and looks back at the soldiers. I've never seen his face so composed. It chills me.

The man with the cramps looks like he's about to cry as he tries to limp back toward the door. Mali comes to his assistance, offering him her arm to lean on. The driver stands in front of the soldier who had earlier pointed his gun at us.

"Cramps," he explains frantically, his hands jabbing the air as he speaks. "The man is suffering cramps and needed to get out."

David hurries over, calling out something in Hebrew. The soldier yells something back at him, and David suddenly turns on his heel, grabs Mali's arm, and leads her back into the van.

"Why are you back here?" somebody yells. "Speak to them!"

"He called us traitors," David replies, "and threatened to imprison the driver and that man if we didn't get back in."

"Your ID!" the soldier demands.

The driver pulls his wallet out from his pants and produces his card.

The soldier looks at it and then throws it back at the driver. He then walks over toward the man with the cramps.

"What problem?" he yells, towering over the man.

"Cramps," the man splutters. "I suffer cramps. There was no room —"

"You not leave van!" He slaps the man in the face. The impact propels the man a step backward. He cries out, raising his hand to his cheek.

"You want trouble?" the soldier yells.

The man stands silent, his eyes fixed on the ground. I want to vomit.

The other soldier approaches. The two soldiers converse quickly in Hebrew and the second soldier says: "It's OK. Fix cramps quick. Then back in van." His voice is stern but gentle.

Somebody cheers. Another claps. "What a good man he is!" somebody exclaims.

"He is so caring compared to the other one," another cries.

"That soldier was nice, wasn't he?" I say to Raghib after everybody has calmed down and quiet has descended over the van.

"I'm reminded of a story I read once when I was a child," Raghib says in a low voice. "Do you want to hear it, Hayaat?" Seeing me nod, he continues. "Once upon a time a hunter went out to the woods to hunt. In the woods, he saw a tree full of birds. He shot at them and many fell. Some were dead and some were wounded. He began to pick up the dead birds and to kill the wounded ones with his knife. While he was busy at his task, a few teardrops came to his eyes because of the cold. Two wounded birds were watching and waiting their turn. One said to the other: 'This hunter has a good heart. Look at his eyes, he is weeping for us.' The other bird said: 'Forget his eyes. Look at his hands.'"

FOURTEEN

Fifteen minutes pass. The man is pleased to announce that his cramps have gone. Several people praise God. Several curse Middle Eastern summers. Some offer him advice on how to increase magnesium in the blood.

We wait bottled up in the service van like the bubbles in a shaken can of fizzy drink.

Twenty-five minutes. Somebody remarks that it's odd to experience cramps in this heat. They usually occur in cold weather, don't they?

Half an hour. David and Mali's heritage is discovered. Oh, the excitement! Peace activists! Israeli peace activists! Such courage, such integrity. Demands for David and Mali to share their stories. Abu Jaffar, a fruit grocer, offers David and Mali some apples and pears from the boxes he has squeezed under his seat and balanced on his lap.

"*Itfadalo.* You are welcome," he says, urging them to eat. So they crunch on an apple and pear each, and we hear about the time they helped a family harvest their fruit orchards in the face of settlers who had tried to prevent them from entering their land. Some trees poisoned. Some shots fired. Then there was the time Um Mazen's house was demolished because she had no permit. They could not stop the demolition. "Actually, maybe that was not such an interesting story to tell," they remark. "What about the summer camp for Israeli and Palestinian children in Jaffa?"

"What a lovely idea!"

"This is what we need more of!"

"Yes, the children spent one week together on the beach, at historical sites, in the bazaars, playing sports, doing arts and crafts."

"Good. Good. Very good."

I try not to be jealous.

An hour. "Could we not open the windows any farther?"

"No, that is as far as they open."

"Well then, forget the flies and peace talks."

One hour and ten minutes. A signal. A soldier flicks his finger and our driver laughs and turns the ignition on. The service rolls forward a few feet, and then the driver is ordered to stop. The ignition is turned off.

"Play the *oud*!"

Marwan beams. But then we realize there's no room for we're squashed, squashed, squashed.

I stare at a small group of blindfolded men crouched on the ground. It seems such a normal sight because their presence doesn't raise a stir among the passengers in the van.

I wonder what the men have done. It can't be too serious as there's only one soldier standing guard over them and he doesn't look too concerned. Have they been caught with the wrong papers? The possibility sends a shiver through my body, given that we're about to do the same thing: to try and enter Jerusalem.

*   *   *

Two hours. It's now three o'clock.

Marwan has dozed off, his head rolling sideways and forward. The sun swells. There are no white or brown faces, just red ones. Samy fidgets as best as he can. I try to count the number of stripes on Raghib's shirt.

We will ourselves to be patient. I marvel at how many people trust in God when all I can think about is stabbing the soldiers' eyes out with their black sunglasses and quenching my thirst with one of Abu Jaffar's pears. Mali marvels, too, but for different reasons. During a conversation about her nephew's Bar Mitzvah, she somehow reveals that she's an agnostic. The passengers are suddenly in a frenzy.

"But you're Jewish!"

"*Ya* Mali, give thanks to Him who shaped you in your mother's womb."

"So what do you say when you stub your toe?" That's Samy, who dislikes church but believes in God in the same way I dislike school but believe in education.

Mali admits to saying "oh my God" in times of crisis or toe-stubbing. Samy looks triumphant. "Aha! So you do believe in God!"

"Yes! Yes! Good point, *ya* Samy," Grace cries.

"He got you!" somebody exclaims with glee.

Mali's crinkled eyes sparkle as she giggles. "You all sound like Orthodox Jews. Perhaps you might have more in common with them than I do! If there is a God, he certainly has the best lawyers sitting here in this bus."

"But there are no lawyers here," Samy says, looking puzzled. "Is anybody here a lawyer?"

"Teacher!"

"Glassmaker!"

"Engineer!"

"Student!"

"Bored housewife," one woman says, provoking laughter among the passengers.

I stare at Mali, curious to meet an agnostic for the first time in my life. She notices me staring and smiles. Not wanting to be impolite, I explain to her that I've been staring because she's an agnostic and not because I want to make her feel uncomfortable. There's something about Mali I really like — she always seems to have a big, fat laugh itching to escape from her crooked, pink mouth. Before she can answer, Samy dives in.

"Yes, but we proved she's not an agnostic, Hayaat! She fell over her words and can't pull them back into her mouth now. They're out there with witnesses who can all testify that she calls on God when she stubs her toe."

"My goodness, Samy!" Mali exclaims. "It turns out we do have a lawyer in the bus after all."

Samy still thinks she's a *Shabak* agent. Maybe that's why he tries to hide the sudden glow in his cheeks.

The line of cars builds up and moves slowly. Sometimes there's no action. No papers being checked, no cars being allowed through, the soldiers standing around like bored employees, perhaps grumbling to one another about low wages or annoying bosses.

We're at the mercy of their moods. The waiting isn't nearly as frustrating as being ignored.

An old man onboard a service directly in front of us suddenly disembarks. His tall, thin frame is supported by a walking stick.

"That's it," David roars. "Mali, come on, get the camera out. They can't touch us."

Some people cheer as David and Mali climb down and walk toward the soldiers, their cameras visible around their necks. I look at Samy, who is following David's and Mali's every step. There's a confused expression on his face.

The old man walks purposefully toward the huddle of soldiers standing at a distance from the blindfolded men. David and Mali follow. We all watch nervously. Those few passengers who are able, lean their heads out of the open windows to listen.

A young soldier turns toward the man and orders him back into the van. The old man stops, fixes the soldier with a stare, and, to our astonishment, refuses.

"Is he senile?"

"Somebody talk to him!"

"David and Mali must do something!"

"Wait! Look!"

The soldier appears startled. The two other soldiers look on in confusion. The old man demands that the passengers be granted permission to disembark. The soldier again orders the old man to return to the service, this time in a gentle tone. The old man stands defiantly and refuses. The tension is palpable. David and Mali step in, raising their cameras at the soldiers. The soldiers look uncomfortable and appear to be demanding David and Mali put their cameras away. David and Mali stand firm. It's like watching a mime.

After a few tense moments, the soldier relents. He sends the old man away with a dismissive wave. The old man seems unperturbed by this indignity. I look on in disbelief as he makes his way back to the service and motions for those onboard to disembark. The door flings open and the passengers pour out. The three soldiers run over, crying out: "Only women and children!" The men stay on and David and Mali snap away with their cameras. The old man ignores the orders and stands leaning against the service. The soldiers don't approach him. One of them glares at David and Mali.

Our driver opens the door of our van and Raghib motions for me to step out. I follow after Grace and four other women, feeling guilty that the men are forced to remain inside. Samy seems unsure whether he should stay with the men or disembark with the women. But the prospect of fresh air is too tempting, and he steps down and joins me.

"Is the jar still in one piece?" he asks.

I open my bag, retrieve it, and display it to him. "Not a scratch," I boast. "If it had been with you, it would have probably smashed. Boys are always rough."

Samy gives me a look of mock indignation and grabs the jar out of my hand, crouching on the ground and scooping soil into it with his bare hands. "I have an idea," he says as he proceeds to fill the jar. I crouch down next to him.

"We'll fill a jar for each part of the journey. This is the jar of the soil at Container checkpoint. Next, a jar of the soil of the checkpoint into Jerusalem. Then a jar of the soil of your grandmother's village. She can put them all beside each other on her mantelpiece."

Samy tightens the lid on the filled jar and, as we stand up, the soldier whose order had been disobeyed by the old man approaches, demanding to see all our papers.

He examines people's cards and papers dexterously, using his walkie-talkie to cross-check certain names with the border police. His eyes eventually focus on me and I hand him my birth certificate. I look up into his eyes. *Cough and he'll break out in a rash and do cartwheels around the checkpoint,* I say to myself. I cough. He doesn't cartwheel. Or break out in a rash. I cough again, and he asks me why I'm traveling alone. I explain that I'm visiting family in Abu Dis and cough some more. He hands my papers back to me and moves on to Samy.

It's just the way it is with Samy. He infuriates adults even without saying a word. His very presence seems a deliberate insolence. The cocky tilt of his head, the nonchalant, sometimes contemptuous way he looks through them instead of at them. Samy stands, pigeon-chested, staring at the soldier as his papers are scrutinized. The soldier reads through Samy's birth certificate and then looks down to find Samy's stare has not broken. He announces Samy's name into the walkie-talkie, and Samy stares on.

"And why you traveling alone and not with parents?" the soldier demands as he waits for a response from the other end of the walkie-talkie. He has an irritated look on his face. The kind our teachers often have when dealing with Samy.

"Because you killed one and imprisoned the other," Samy replies.

The soldier blinks violently. I cough and cough but to no avail. Samy stares up into the soldier's eyes. Any haziness in Samy's eyes has gone. There's nothing but clear detachment.

A voice floats out of the walkie-talkie and the soldier raises an eyebrow. "So you the son of a prisoner?" he asks in a tone that doesn't invite a response. "And where you going?"

"Abu Dis," Samy says after a long pause. He just can't manage the humble tone. His voice oozes contempt.

"Not thinking of being terrorist like your father, I hope."

"He's a hero," Samy shoots back.

The soldier suddenly grabs the jar from Samy's hand and raises it close to his face to examine it.

"And what is this?"

"My land."

The soldier bobs down to Samy's eye level. Samy's eyes are impenetrable as he maintains his stony stare. But then I notice his hands by his sides. They're trembling.

The soldier rises, glances at Samy, and then smashes the jar onto the ground. Samy's trembling hands clench into tight fists.

"If you think you are man," the soldier says calmly, "you welcome join men inside service. Otherwise, you stay out here with the women and children. I leave to you choose."

He smiles gloatingly and turns his back on Samy, moving on to the next person. Samy looks at the broken pieces of glass on the ground before him. He looks up at the steps of the service, then at the women and children crowded outside. His shoulders slump and that hard, defiant expression collapses into defeat and shame.

I walk up beside him. "Samy, we're in Palestine," I say, feigning a light tone. "There are hummus jars everywhere, remember?"

He grunts and turns away from me.

FIFTEEN

Some of us are eventually allowed through, Samy and I included. Others are not.

Those allowed to continue take their seats on the service. With some passengers turned away, there's more room. Our driver runs the engine, fidgeting impatiently in his seat. We approach the iron gate slowly. A soldier flicks his finger to signal that we can pass.

We've been at the Container checkpoint for just over two and a half hours.

My bladder starts to throb again. It screams at me, threatens to humiliate me, pleads with me that the occupation is none of its business. I beg it to understand, but it refuses to stop throbbing.

I'm now worried about whether I'll make it to a toilet. Not to mention the overall delay. We'll be expected home from school soon and our absence will raise an alarm. As the service's last stop is the town of Abu Dis, I decide that when we arrive I'll find a toilet and then telephone home. I'm anxious to find out how Sitti Zeynab is doing.

It's odd. In reality we're less than six miles away from home. For those with blue cards, a car ride of minutes. And yet I feel as though we've journeyed to another country.

We drive through the village of al-Sawahreh. My bladder is giving me last-minute ultimatums, and I cry out for the driver to stop the service and allow me to disembark. One glance at my face, beaded with sweat and pinched with agony, and he agrees. I sprint to the nearest shop — a convenience store — enter, and run to the desk. I plead with the owner to allow me to use the toilet. She does. The relief is overwhelming.

I reboard the bus and we continue on to the town of Abu Dis, under the Mount of Olives. The driver makes a sharp U-turn, narrowly missing a taxi, a boy selling safety pins, and a sleepy-looking grocer. Having been through Wadi al-Nar, I don't even flinch.

"Al-Quds," I whisper under my breath, pressing my nose up against the window. My stomach winds itself into tight knots as I take in a panoramic view of the holy city of Jerusalem and the surrounding green rolling hills filled with olive trees. I suddenly understand that there is dignity in being able to claim heritage, in being able to derive identity from a rocky hill, a winding mountain road. Sitti Zeynab's village has never stopped calling her, beckoning her to return home. Her soul is stamped into these hills, and I feel her presence as strongly as if she were standing on the peak of one of the mountains.

"I went to a wedding in Abu Dis," Sitti Zeynab once told me. "Back in the day when travel was not so difficult. Your mother will be very angry with me for telling you this story, but that's what grandmothers are for. The groom's name was Husni but some weeks after the wedding he was called Abu Ades, Father of Lentils, and nobody ever called him Husni again.

"Abu Ades had decided to take on a second wife because he was bored with his first. He was a donkey, *ya* Hayaat, abusing religion like that, but that is life and the way of men with no brains.

"His first wife, Lara, was thirty-nine, had long hair down to her waist and magnificent brown eyes. The new bride was Fatima from Nablus, and she had blue eyes, fair hair, and was eighteen years old. She was an orphan and had been raised by her great-aunt. Lara had not even a pumpkin seed's worth of pity. She was furious and vowed revenge. Lara insisted on attending the wedding. She didn't leave the dance floor and danced around the bride and groom, clapping vigorously, performing ululations, the *zaghareet*. She laughed and cheered and we all thought she had gone mad. That the donkey had finally turned her into a lunatic.

"What I remember is her chewing down hard on a piece of gum the whole night. The louder she clapped, the more her jaw worked, as though all her anger was being channeled into gnawing that piece of chewing gum between her teeth. But a plan was swimming in her head, we later learned.

"A week or so after the wedding she went into the kitchen in the middle of the night and cooked lentil soup. I know you do not like lentil soup but that is beside the point. For hours she let it boil and boil.

Finally, it spewed over the edges of the pot, a horrible, rotting smell climbing out of it. Do you know that smell?"

I nodded, scrunching my nose up.

"As the bride and groom lay asleep, Lara snuck into their room and poured a trail of the sticky brown lentil mess right under the bride's bottom. A little smudged on the bride's white satin nightgown, and Lara paused to grin to herself."

"How do you know she paused to grin to herself?"

Sitti Zeynab frowned. "Lara has retold this story so many times we all feel we were in the room with her. Anyway, wouldn't you pause and grin to yourself if you were getting revenge on your donkey husband?"

"I suppose. But I feel sorry for Fatima. It's not her fault."

Sitti Zeynab shrugged. "That's life. Now let me continue. Lara left the sleeping couple and went to bed. She awoke some hours later to the sound of her husband and his new bride screeching with horror. She rushed to the room and was delighted with the scene that greeted her. Her husband stood pointing in disgust at the bride.

"'The bride has soiled herself!' he exclaimed over and over again. And the poor bride looked behind and, apparently too intimidated — and stupid in my opinion — to accuse Lara, covered her face with shame.

"The donkey divorced Fatima and she returned to Nablus, a divorcée with blue eyes and fair hair. From then on Lara apparently only had to say jump and her husband would ask how high. And that is the story of Abu Ades, and you must now swear never to tell your mother you heard about it from me."

The driver suddenly slams his foot on the brake, our path cut by a bored-looking pony lazily ambling its way across the road and then negotiating its large rear end down through the sloping backyard of a house.

David and Mali turn around in their seats to face Samy and me.

"It's beautiful, isn't it?" David says.

I nod shyly. Samy looks at David and then impolitely averts his eyes.

"Where are you going?" Mali asks.

"To Jerusalem," I reply. "To my grandmother's village." They want to hear more so I tell them about our plans, conveniently omitting the part about our families having no idea where we are.

Samy decides to provide further embellishment by adding that our families have "sent us."

"But do you have the papers to enter?" David asks.

"*Bin kalb* to the papers," he says coolly. "We will get in."

I take out a photograph of Sitti Zeynab. "It was taken the day I was born," I explain, passing them the photograph. "That bundle she's holding, the one with the monkey face? That's me." I smile.

Mali politely comments that Sitti Zeynab looks sweet, despite the fact that my grandmother stares stony-faced into the camera, as though not smiling will attach an air of dignity and status to her portrait.

"If she met you she would curse you and your ancestors," I say, giggling.

They raise their eyebrows. "How flattering," David says.

"But she doesn't mean it. She told me so herself. She says we all laugh the same. . . . Do you want to come with us? You said you were going to Jerusalem."

Samy hits me in the side and asks David and Mali to put their fingers in their ears as he wants to talk about them but can't do so given their command of Arabic.

"Oh, so you don't trust us?" Mali asks, her mouth twitching.

Samy shrugs but doesn't reply. His brashness never ceases to amaze me. Even more amazing is the graciousness with which Mali and David raise their fingers to their ears. They look at us, index fingers wedged into the sides of their heads, lopsided grins on their faces.

"What's wrong?" I ask quietly.

"We've come this far on our own. We don't need grown-ups. Let alone ones who could be agents."

"They're not agents, Samy. I like them and they can help us."

We argue in hushed tones for several more moments, Samy submitting the basis upon which he considers them to be undercover spies, me throwing him a long list of synonyms for the word *paranoid*.

He huffs and puffs. I cross my arms over my chest, and David and Mali look on from their soundproofed positions. I win the argument because Samy can be stubborn with everybody in the world except me. Once

I've assured him that I'll report any spylike activity to him, we agree to invite them, and I motion for David and Mali to remove their fingers from their ears.

"So what's the problem?" David asks good-naturedly.

"If you'd like to . . . if you're not busy . . . you're welcome to come with us to Jerusalem."

They're happy to accompany us. I beam. Samy grunts.

The service stops at a taxi junction and we all disembark. Marwan nods good-bye to Raghib and Grace and shakes David's and Mali's hands.

Then he turns to Samy and me, his earphones still dangling down his chest, his *oud* case propped under his arm.

"There's no war in music," he says softly. "Remember that, yes?" He winks at us and walks away, his pointy leather shoes kicking up the dusty road.

We wait for a service to take us to al-Ayzariyyah. We stand at the top of a dusty incline lined with white limestone houses and apartment buildings, the flat roofs decorated with TV antennas and water tanks.

Mali offers us her cell phone while we wait. Samy and I stand to the side and I call home first. Jihan answers, and my stomach lurches with both the fear of being caught and ordered to return and a longing to be back in the safety of my home.

"Jihan? It's me. How is Sitti?"

"Where are you? If you're playing with Samy, I'll throttle you when you get home! Mama and Baba leave me in charge and you decide to come home late from school!"

After I assuage her anger and feed her a story about *dabka* practice, she tells me that Sitti Zeynab has just arrived home.

"Is she OK?"

"Yes, just weak and tired."

I tell Jihan to reassure Sitti Zeynab that I have a surprise for her, but Jihan swiftly cuts me off as Ahmad is trying to get through on her cell.

Samy's conversation with Amto Christina is much quicker. He simply reassures her *dabka* practice will still allow him to make it in time for volunteering at church and then he hangs up.

"I doubt you'll make it in time."

He grins. "Yes, I know."

"We're crazy. Look at the time. It's past four. We haven't even entered Jerusalem yet." I raise my head to the sky and sigh. "Even if we make it to Sitti Zeynab's village and somehow manage to get back, we won't be home before night." I shudder. "Do you know something? I think I'm more terrified of how Mama will react than I am of getting caught."

"You have a point," Samy says thoughtfully. "Your mom is scary. But so what? Don't tell me you want to back out now?"

"Of course not."

"Then what are you talking about?"

"What do you mean?"

"About your mom? What do you mean?"

"I'm just telling you how I feel."

Samy looks bewildered. "Why?"

"Oh, for God's sake," I say, walking back to David and Mali. "You really can be an idiot."

"At least my head's screwed on straight," he calls out.

SIXTEEN

We board yet another service. The driver speeds down the streets and then takes the al-Ayzariyyah road. Wasim had explained that al-Ayzariyyah's main road connects to the Jerusalem–Jericho road and that within minutes we can reach the Old City. My heart skips a beat as I realize how close we are. What had seemed impossible only hours ago is now so close I can practically feel the soil running through my fingers.

I wonder what Sitti Zeynab's house will look like after all these years. Will the village itself lie neglected and homesick for its owners? I can't bear to imagine that Jewish family from Europe living in Sitti Zeynab's home.

We drive on. David doesn't like silence. Mali doesn't seem to mind it. Samy and I never feel the need to make conversation unless we have something to say.

David turns to face us and asks us to tell him about our lives. I wonder where to start. Mama says she felt me kick her in her stomach when she was a full five months into her pregnancy, although Baba attributes the alleged incident to a late-night plate of falafel. I might tell them about the time I tripped and fell over in a *dabka* performance at school and ran off the stage in tears. Baba took me and my friends for ice cream afterward and boasted to them how proud he was of me. I might tell them about the time Mama accidentally burped loudly when Ahmad and his parents visited to ask for Jihan's hand in marriage and then blamed the offensive belch on me. Instead, though, I tell them about Jihan's wedding plans and how Mama has started drugging Jihan to prepare her for marriage.

"What do you mean, drugging?" David asks in shock. Mali stares at me, her mouth open.

I explain that I've seen Jihan swallow a tiny tablet every evening, and that Mama has been going to great lengths to remind Jihan to take the tablet at the same time each day. "But Sitti Zeynab disapproves," I add. "She says it's silly to wait and that it's easier to cope when you're young. I don't know, though. I suppose it depends on the illness. They refuse to speak to me about it and insist I should stay out of adult affairs, which is ridiculous because as much as Jihan annoys me, she's my sister. I mean, I have the right to know why marrying Ahmad is making her sick."

David and Mali exchange a look that makes me suspect there's laughter dancing in their eyes. Samy offers the opinion that if Jihan is so sick and requires daily medication, then perhaps she should not be trying to lose weight. "She should preserve her energy."

David then moves on to Samy, not realizing he would have more luck eliciting information from a statue. The only person Samy speaks to is me. And even then we rarely discuss anything personal. Samy meets David's eager friendliness with aloofness. "I like soccer."

It's painful to watch David try to draw out Samy further. Of course I know that Samy isn't going to reveal too much to people he thinks may be *Shabak* agents. What I don't know is that David is aware of the problem too.

"We aren't agents, Samy," he says in a gentle tone.

"Agents?" Mali cries. "Huh!" She slaps her hand on her thigh and laughs loudly.

Samy is outraged and his face flushes cherry red.

"You were supposed to block your ears! You cheated!"

"Sorry but I clean my ears regularly, Samy," David says, grinning. "There wasn't enough wax in them to block out your voice."

Samy folds his arms across his chest and purses his lips in anger. "Well, I'm entitled to think what I want."

"Samy," Mali says kindly, "you can trust us."

David retrieves an envelope of photographs from his bag. "Here, have a look at these."

Samy takes the envelope and slowly flips through the photos. I lean close to him to look as well. In the first photo, a bulldozer is parked in front of a house. David is lying down on the ground in front of it with four other people. Flipping over, David is being dragged by a soldier. Next: Mali and David are eating at the table of a Palestinian family, everybody grinning at the camera. Then: a group shot of Palestinian children, men, women, and David and Mali, arms all linked as they stand in front of Al-Rowwad Cultural and Theatre

Training Centre in Aida camp. Last: Mali stands in between a soldier and a man in a *keffiyeh*, Mali obviously in an argument with the soldier, her hands in the air, her crazy curls lifted in the wind.

Samy hands back the photos. "They're . . . nice. . . ." he says in a subdued voice, avoiding eye contact.

They're not just nice. They're marvelous.

"So tell us something about your life," I say to Mali.

She tilts her head to the side and grins. "Hmm . . . OK. Well, I love chocolate. I write a to-do list every morning and usually do nothing on it. And I have a gorgeous dog named Missy."

"Where do you live?" Samy asks.

"New York."

"Are you and David married?"

"Yes."

"Where did you meet?"

"Was it love at first sight?"

"Is David an atheist?"

"What do Jews do on the Sabbath?"

Mali and David laugh.

"Slow down," Mali says.

"OK, my question first!" Samy says.

"Well, we met at a friend's birthday party."

"I liked Mali's curly hair. It was crazy. It was *like* at first sight."

"Oh no, mister," Mali cries, playfully hitting his arm, "you're not getting off that easily. You confessed to me that you were besotted the first time you laid eyes on me."

"There's a rule about repeating that kind of information, you know."

"Where was the party?" I ask.

"It was a beach party in California. David was wearing the funniest clothes. A Hawaiian floral shirt with bright yellow board shorts, socks, and sneakers! He had his hair in a ponytail like it is now but he was wearing a headband."

"Why were you dressed like a girl?" Samy asks incredulously.

"Hey! Everybody said I looked very trendy."

Mali grins at us. "Well, he did look very cool. Weird, but trendy."

"Have you got children?"

"No."

"Well, you better hurry," Samy says flatly. "You're already pretty old."

David laughs. "Hey, we're in our late thirties."

"So you see my point," Samy says solemnly.

Suddenly, Mali cries out: "Oh no!"

The driver swerves to the side of the road and turns the ignition off. Arching my neck, I look ahead. The road has come to a sudden halt. A six-foot-high concrete wall, topped with rolls of barbed wire and stretching as far as the eye can see from right to left, cuts across the tarmac, blocking the way in a colossal concrete T-junction. About half-a-dozen service cabs and taxis are parked haphazardly in front of the wall, the drivers leaning against their vehicles, smoking and gossiping.

"For God's sake . . ." David mutters, shaking his head in despair.

"Now what do we do?" Samy groans.

The driver has opened the door and the other passengers disembark. When the four of us are still in our seats he turns around and says: "Come on. Last stop."

"But what do we do?" I ask, standing up hastily. "We want to go to Jerusalem."

The driver lets out a harsh laugh and points out of the window. "As you see."

"But this road is supposed to take us to the Jerusalem–Jericho road," Samy says.

The thick eyebrows on the driver's round, sunburned face arch in surprise. "What are you talking about? That time is long gone."

"But we thought this service would take us," Samy says.

"What did I just say?" the driver cries impatiently. "The Wall is here now! Now, *yallah*, I have to get to an appointment."

We walk toward the convoy of service cabs and taxis. I glance at the stretch of Wall alongside us. It's obviously incomplete, the vertical blocks unequal in length. Rocks, concrete blocks, and graffitied boulders are strewn haphazardly in front of it. The ground is dusty and gray, rubbish and building debris lying around. The red spray-painted words

AL-AYZARIYYAH GHETTO are splattered on a concrete slab.

As we approach the cluster of taxis and service cabs, a flurry of drivers flocks to us, their cries filling the air.

"I have air-conditioning!"

"My cab is clean!"

"Discount! I'll give you a discount!"

They encircle us, their eyes pleading with us to choose them, like hungry, squawking seagulls.

David holds his hands up and motions for them to be quiet. "We want to get to Jerusalem. How do we get there?"

"It depends. What passes do you have?"

"We're here on foreign passports but we're traveling with our two friends here," David says.

Impressed by David's fluent Arabic, the drivers give him winning smiles.

"Well, you'll pass through the checkpoints easily. But are they West Bankers?"

"Yes. But we want to travel with them."

"I will take you, my friend," one says.

"No, I will," another insists.

"*Ya zalami,* just tell us how to get there first!" Mali says, her use of colloquial Arabic making the drivers all beam and coo with excitement. "Tell us *exactly* how to get there," she says. "No surprises."

After lavishing praise on her Arabic, one man says: "You drive to the checkpoint at the settlement of Ma'ale Adumim. Then you turn around and head to the A-Zaim checkpoint. Then to French Hill and then to East Jerusalem. But these two kids won't get in."

"Oof!" Samy exclaims, throwing his hands in the air. "I am carsick from all this traveling!"

"East Jerusalem is minutes away, isn't it?" David asks.

"Yes, it's on the other side of this Wall," one driver says matter-of-factly.

"Well, how long will it take by car?" Mali asks in a frustrated tone.

Various time frames are hurled about and another argument erupts over which of the numerous contingencies is least time-consuming. Finally, there's agreement on an estimate of forty-five minutes to an hour. Samy and I are sick of listening to the adults and squat on our haunches beside David and Mali.

The drivers' eyes all look down and focus on Samy and me.

"So why are you traveling with these two kids?" one man asks, rubbing his chin. "Are you trying to smuggle them in? To a hospital or something? I've heard of this happening. Maybe for the girl's face?"

I bury his comment inside and then block out the sound of Mali and David negotiating a route with the drivers. I turn my head to a section of the Wall that's been obscured by the cars, when I notice a plump woman wearing a bottle-green shirt, black pants, and green *hijab* standing against the concrete in front of a number of rocks and boulders that have been placed one on top of the other as if to form a small staircase. The woman's arms are casually folded in front of her. She's laughing and joking with a woman dressed in a black *abaya*, burgundy *hijab*, and brown open-toed summer shoes. The latter leans one palm against the Wall as she tries to maneuver her heavy body over the steps, the other arm stretched out in midair for balance. I walk over toward them, Samy following close behind me.

The woman in the black *abaya* laughs out loud, telling her friend what a tease she is, watching her fumble over the rocks like a child in a playground.

"Show us your legs, *yallah*, show us!" the woman says as her friend hitches her *abaya* up to her knees and tries to step up. But underneath she wears black leggings and laughs back at the woman, throwing a backward glance at the men huddled around the service cabs.

I watch in disbelief as the middle-aged woman struggles to climb over the Wall. When she has perched herself at the top, like Humpty Dumpty, she shrieks. "I'm scared! There's nothing to step down onto."

"Call out for help!"

The woman calls over to the other side, "Girls! *Allah yerda alaikum*, God be pleased with you. Help me over!"

The woman holds her grip at the top and then moments later she flips over the Wall, releasing a shriek as she does.

Her friend reaches for her cell phone and dials. "Najwa!" she shrieks into the phone. "Najwa! Have you broken your neck? No? It's fine. Good. *Alhamdulilah!* Yes, I'll see you at seven. *Yallah, assalamu alaikom!*"

The woman turns around, hitches her bag onto one shoulder, and begins to walk away.

"Excuse me please," I say, intercepting her. "Where did your friend go?"

The woman's green eyes seem to be drowning in the pudginess of her face. She studies my face and then smiles. "To Ras al-Amoud."

"Do you mean East Jerusalem?" Samy asks.

She nods and explains that her friend, Najwa, has an appointment and won't make it in time if she catches a service. As the Wall is, in its temporary form, only six feet high, people are climbing it to avoid the long detour. Apparently the soldiers sometimes turn a blind eye. It's a matter of chance. Samy and I decide that we prefer to test our luck and enter East Jerusalem in a couple of minutes rather than take the safer option of catching a cab but adding up to an hour or so to our trip.

"Anyway," Samy reflects, "even if we went by the road, we don't have the blue pass to enter at the checkpoint. So from now on we *have* to move illegally."

We call David and Mali to our side. They plead with us to take a service, but once they realize Samy and I can't be persuaded otherwise, they decide they'll jump the Wall with us.

We stand in front of the Wall and it hits me. If we cross now, we'll be illegally entering Jerusalem. I think of Sitti Zeynab, Mama, and Baba, and I feel instant guilt, knowing how angry and afraid they'd be if they knew what I'm about to do. I push such thoughts out of my head.

David insists on going first. "Just in case there are soldiers on the other side," he says.

Some of the cabdrivers gather together in a throng and watch us curiously as they smoke, yelling out conflicting instructions on how to mount the Wall and jump down.

"A kid broke his back the other day," one calls out. "So be careful."

"Just what we needed to hear," Samy mutters.

David offers to take my backpack. He hitches it onto his back and Shrek's face grins at the drivers. With his lean legs, David has no problem jumping the Wall and is over in a matter of moments.

Mali's cell phone rings and she answers. It's safe to jump.

I go next, balancing myself on the rocks, grateful I'm wearing sneakers and jeans. I tread carefully, aware that the slightest awkwardness could result in a twisted ankle. I stretch my body and extend my arms up, grabbing the top of the Wall. I pull myself up and use all my energy to swing one leg over. I hesitate for a moment and then lean forward on the narrow, flat surface, flattening my stomach against the top and straddling my legs. I look over at the side where Samy and Mali stand. Samy is gazing up at me, concern in his eyes. Beads of sweat drop from my forehead and my arms tremble.

I can hear Mali and Samy yelling out words of encouragement. I focus on keeping my balance and peer over the other side, where David is waiting for me.

"I'll catch you. Don't be afraid," he says calmly. He stands with his legs apart, bracing himself.

I bite down on my lip, slowly flip my leg over, and grab on to the edge of the Wall as tightly as possible. I'm dangling now and I look down, trying to ascertain David's position. He calls out directions and

I count to three and let go, my hands scraping against the coarse surface of the concrete. He catches me and we tumble onto the ground. Our eyes meet and we burst into laughter.

I examine my stinging hands. They're scratched and bloodied but I don't care.

Mali's head peeks over the top of the Wall. I call out to her to trust in God and enjoy hearing her cackle as she negotiates the top of the Wall.

Samy follows moments later. He refuses David's assistance, jumps, falls to the ground, and then hops up, dusting the dirt off his clothes. He kisses his cross and then steps toward me. Our faces simultaneously erupt into wide grins.

"We made it," I whisper, raising my trembling hands to wipe the grimy sweat off my face.

"I always knew we would," he says with a lopsided grin and then grabs my hand. We dance the *dabka* in a small circle, and Mali and David look on, laughing. Samy stops, seizes David's hand, and orders him to take Mali's.

"Come on!" Samy cries with a cheeky grin. "Every *Shabak* agent knows how to dance the *dabka*!"

SEVENTEEN

We're in East Jerusalem. Ras al-Amoud is a mere mile from the Old City, where we can catch a service from the bus stand in front of Damascus Gate to Sitti Zeynab's village in West Jerusalem.

It's important that Samy and I avoid attracting the suspicion of any roaming border police. We decide that Samy and I will hide and David and Mali will head to the nearest service cab stop and inquire about transport to the Old City and whether there's any additional security today.

Samy and I crouch low in an alley adjoining a cluster of shops. We crouch next to some boxes at the opening of the alley so that we still have a view of the street.

"I'll admit something to you, Hayaat."

"This is a first."

"Then enjoy it. . . . I don't suspect David and Mali anymore. In fact, they're two of the nicest people I've ever met."

"I think so too," I say as I cup my chin in my hand, lean my elbow on my thigh, and examine the faces of Palestinians walking along the street. They clutch their children's hands, hold bags of shopping, dangle a cigarette from their mouths, or swing their arms briskly. The distinction between blue and green has never seemed so artificial.

We're bored and start a game of I Spy.

"Something beginning with S," I say in English.

"We do this in English?"

"Yes. We have to practice."

"OK. Easy! Soldier?"

I shake my head. "I can't see a soldier anyway."

"Sun?"

"No."

"Sea?"

"Sea? Where is the sea, *ya* Samy?"

Samy shrugs and reverts to Arabic. "I've run out of S words in English. That's all I know."

I grin. "Ostaza Mariam would be proud."

"Well?"

"Star," I say triumphantly.

"But it's daytime."

"The sun is a star."

"But I said 'sun'!"

I shrug my shoulders. "You have to guess the *exact* word."

"That's stupid."

We survey the street. Positioned diagonally from our hiding spot is an imposing sandstone villa. The front courtyard is shaded by trees, some of the branches lazily leaning against the green wrought-iron front gate. The facade is long with a square flat-roofed tower jutting up in the center, below which stands a grand, white double door. On each side of the door are sandstone arched windows with white decorative wrought-iron grates covering them.

"Nice house, isn't it?" I say.

"When I'm a famous soccer player and you're my personal assistant managing my ten bank accounts — I can see you rolling your eyes, you know — I'll have a house five times the size of that with a television in each room and not one statue of Jesus on the walls.

What do you think my aunt and uncle would say to that?"

"I can think of plenty of things I could say to that."

At the front of the house I spot three children, two boys and one girl, huddled together. The boys wear black dress hats and suits. One has long ginger curls dangling down the sides of his head. The other has shorter black curls. The girl wears a long skirt and long-sleeved shirt, buttoned to her neck. Her hair is pulled back into a low ponytail. She's holding on to the green front gate, leaning back and laughing at the boys.

"They must be from the new settlement," I say in a low voice, anger rising within me as I think of the Israeli-only compound illegally built on Palestinian land.

Samy stares out at them with curious eyes. "I wonder why the boys wear their hair long at the front."

We watch them, half fascinated, half afraid. I gaze upon these children and feel like a pot of simmering water into which Mama has sprinkled a mixture of spices. A pinch of resentment. A dash of curiosity. A sprinkle of jealousy.

We grow restless as we wait for David's and Mali's return. We argue about abandoning our hiding spot and venturing out on our own. I remain while Samy attempts to elicit information about our options from people in the nearby shops. He returns with a replacement jar of hummus (which he has emptied and cleaned out with a tissue) and some information. It's all about luck. We might be stopped. We might not.

A black SUV emerges across the road, parking in front of the children. They hop in, and now I'll never have the chance to talk to them, to tell them my name. If I had, I might have asked them to remember me when they inspect my identity card in five years' time. I might have written down my telephone number and invited them to lunch at my house so I could ask them about their long side-curls and whether they have an Israeli *X Factor.*

David and Mali return, suddenly converts to conservatism.

"It just feels so reckless," Mali says, nervously biting her nails and pacing the alley. "I can't imagine your families would agree to this. And I wouldn't blame them."

"What if you're caught?" David adds solemnly. "The closer you are to West Jerusalem, the riskier it is. We really are so sorry, but you have to face the fact that it's just too dangerous."

I don't bother to argue with them. I have no time for their guilty consciences or adult apprehension. In fact, their reluctance invigorates my determination. I look up at their eyes, so kind and compassionate.

"We'll walk you back to the Wall and help you over," David says.

"Thank you," I hear myself say, "but we'll be fine from here."

"We don't want to leave you," Mali says. "We have a responsibility toward —"

Samy bolts then. "Run, Hayaat!" he shouts as his legs pound the ground, collecting dust behind him.

My eyes meet David's, then Mali's. Their faces explode with the realization: They know I'll follow him almost before I do. I crash through the people walking on the sidewalk and keep my eyes focused on Samy's mane of black hair as I sprint after him. If David and Mali have cried out in response, I don't hear them. I can only hear my footsteps and the furious beat of my heart. I catch up with Samy in a crowded market square. We dissolve into the crowd and are on our own once more.

I'm crazy. It's already so late in the day. We haven't even reached Sitti Zeynab's village, let alone worked out how we'll get back and how long it will take. I see Mama and Baba, sitting in our living room, Mama's shrill voice bouncing off the walls as she takes her frustration out on Baba. He's silent, infuriating Mama even further. Jihan is moaning about how I've ruined her wedding plans. I am flooded with guilt. The last thing I want to do is worry my family, but if they knew how much Sitti Zeynab needs to touch the soil of her village one last time, they would understand.

We decide that it's too risky to continue on foot, so we step into a linen shop and speak to the owner.

"Excuse me," I ask, "can you tell us how we can get to West Jerusalem?"

"Have you got the *hawiya*, the pass?"

We shake our heads.

The woman looks up from the cash register, her thin

eyebrows raised high. She gestures to the man behind the counter who is folding a tablecloth.

"*Ya* Bassam," she says, "these kids want to get to West Jerusalem. They don't have the pass. Shall we check if the limousine is free to escort them?" They both burst out laughing.

We turn on our heels, Samy deliberately knocking over a pile of folded towels on his way.

"Oh, how clumsy of me!" he cries and we run out, the woman's curses sounding in the air.

"Donkeys," Samy mutters when we stop at a corner.

"Let's talk to a taxi driver," I suggest. "One of them would know."

We approach a rake-thin man who sports a neat mustache. His eyelashes are long, giving him an oddly feminine appearance.

"Leave it to me this time," Samy says, stepping in front of me.

"Fine," I say, folding my arms across my chest and looking on.

"Excuse me," Samy says, "my sister and I are trying to find our way to a private hospital in West Jerusalem.

Our aunt is there and we want to see her before she dies. That's what the doctors are predicting, and if we don't have a chance to say good-bye, it will probably ruin our lives forever. Is it possible to sneak in without the pass? Can you tell us how?"

"Must be a close aunt, yes?" the taxi driver says, a twinkle in his eye.

"Oh yes, very," Samy says solemnly. "She raised us. We're very, very close to her. Isn't that right, Hayaat?"

I nod. "Yes. Very close. Samy here is struggling to sleep at night because he's so used to Amto Fifi reading him a bedtime story."

Samy glares at me and I smile innocently.

The taxi driver chuckles. "Come on, kids, I haven't got time for this. I'm waiting around for a fare. Buzz off."

"Please," I beg. "OK, so we lied. . . . But we really need to get there. . . . See my face? I don't like to talk about it but I have to find a specialist." I look up at him, trying to appear as sad as possible.

He coughs, suddenly uncomfortable. "Oh, OK. *Salamtik*, your health. Do you have money?"

We take out our pooled funds and show him.

"There's an Israeli guy, Yossi. He helps us. Smuggles people into West Jerusalem in his car. He'll look after you. Wait here. I'll give him a call."

He steps to the side to make the call.

"What luck!" I exclaim.

"Yeah, well, I was doing fine until you mentioned bedtime stories."

The taxi driver returns. "Yossi will be here in ten minutes."

When he arrives Samy leans close to me. "Can we trust this Yossi guy?"

"Yes," I say firmly, because the alternative is too scary.

Yossi is thin and short, his face angular. He wears a white shirt and when he lifts his arms to scratch his head I notice yellow sweat stains.

"Hello," he says with a broad smile.

"Hello," we reply.

"You have nothing to worry about," he reassures us, his gentle tone inspiring my confidence. "My friends and I do this all the time."

"Have you ever been caught?" Samy asks.

"Not yet, God forbid," he says. "I've got yellow license plates. It should be fine. You're both small so I can easily conceal you."

He recommends we put our papers into our pockets. He places my backpack on the floor of the front passenger seat. He then opens the back door of his white car. A pile of gray blankets is shoved on one side of the backseat, a pile of dolls on the other.

"My daughter's," he says, noticing me looking at them. "She's messy. Like her father."

He instructs us to fold ourselves into the fetal position on the floor and lie motionless if we're stopped. There's plenty of room as the front seats are pushed forward. I curl myself into a ball, my head facing the door. Samy does the same, and Yossi gives us a warning before covering our bodies with the blankets.

"Are you both OK?" he asks.

We reply with a muffled "Yes."

"I'm just going to throw some dolls, clothes, and shoes and things on top of you to make the car look messy." He pauses. "Well, *messier*."

I don't know what's strewn over me, but it's weight-less and doesn't add to my discomfort.

"We'll have dusk on our side," Yossi says as we drive off. He then advises us that in congested traffic he has to refrain from talking so as not to arouse suspicion. "Or I'll look like a madman."

Samy and I are left with our thoughts. My stomach stitches into knots. Curled up like this, feeling every pothole and ditch in the road, guilt and regret continue to prick me, and my earlier confidence seems pathetic and childish. Until this point, I've chosen to suppress the stories of people being beaten, arrested, and impris-oned for sneaking into Jerusalem without a permit. Samy lies curled beside me, silent. Perhaps he, too, understands the enormity of what we're risking. I won-der if our understanding has come too late.

We drive on in silence for ten minutes. My body feels numb and my limbs scream out to me to stretch them.

"We just passed Damascus Gate," Yossi says.

I'm desperate to peek out at the window and see the medieval wall of the Old City that Sitti Zeynab has so often spoken to me about. But then I hear the wailing sirens of police cars. Our car comes to a sudden halt as Yossi slams down on the brakes.

"Oh no!" he cries. "What bad luck you have!"

"What's happening?"

"Have we been caught?"

Samy and I cry out from under our blankets and Yossi swears, hitting his hand on the steering wheel in frustration.

"There's a protest," he says. "Of all days. A big group is blocking the roads. I can't drive through or back." He swerves and stops abruptly. "The jeeps have blocked me. It looks like there are clashes. Your only hope is to rush into the crowd and then lose yourself. Quick! Go now before you're stuck here! Quick! God be with you!"

I fling the blankets off my back. Samy has hurled his off too. He looks at me, his eyes wild with fear, and says: "Don't lose me! Stay close."

On the count of three we throw the doors open. We're in a crowd of protestors, surrounded by military jeeps, police cars, and soldiers. The large crowd chants through megaphones and carries placards and Palestinian flags. We hurl our bodies toward the protestors, running between two soldiers and a jeep and a police car. I look up and catch a glimpse of the wall of the Old City behind me, the sunset collapsing over it. It's breathtaking.

The noise of the protestors is deafening. Samy and I link hands and try to squeeze through the press of people. But the crowd has transformed into a mob, people trampling one another as they work themselves into a frenzy. With each step forward we're pushed two steps back by a wave of men and women, incensed, enraged. A sound grenade explodes and my ears feel as though they've been ripped from the sides of my head. There's a hissing sound from above and a cloud of gas obscures my vision. My eyes sting and I rub furiously at them, dropping Samy's hand. I hear women and men screaming, and I'm bumped and jostled as I try to see. The air is thick with tear gas; my eyes are burning. I can't open them. I stumble forward, crying out Samy's name. Panicked screams are the only reply.

I drop to the ground on my knees. It's too painful to inhale. My entire face is burning now. I try to open my eyes. I see a man collapse beside me. I close my eyes again and lie down on the ground. I hear people crying out warnings. "Run! They're coming!" I can't stop coughing. I try to feel my way forward, touching the cobbled stone streets of Jerusalem.

"Samy!" I scream.

And that's when she visits me. Maysaa, who has swooped out of the shadows of my bedroom at night to haunt me. Maysaa. Who previously averaged ten out of ten in all her mathematics tests and had the fortune to be named the *second*-best *dabka* dancer in our class. Maysaa. Who always made me laugh with her impersonations of our teachers and parents. Who was shot in the forehead and died soaked in a pool of spreading blood mixed with my vomit.

She visits me as I lie on the streets of Jerusalem, and I feel as though Judgment Day has arrived.

We're on our way home from school. We hear that the soldiers have shot a man as punishment for his links to a suicide bomber. Now his family's home is to be demolished as a punishment and warning to all.

"Shall we go and watch? Join the protest?" Maysaa asks. She tells me that we need the soldiers to know we won't be silent. The more voices, the better, she says, and I agree.

I'm curious. I saw a demolition once, but Baba made me leave halfway through it. He said it reminded him of what happened to our home. But I wasn't there to see the bulldozers on our land.

The protestors range in age from about twelve to twenty-five and stand with the dead man's extended family one hundred feet from the bulldozer, singing loudly in protest.

The bulldozer attacks. The dust from the rubble is so thick it rises from the earth like the mist on a cold winter's morning. The sound is terrible. Glass shattering, concrete smacking the earth, people screaming in despair, soldiers yelling out orders for us to stand back. Maysaa grabs on to my arm and then buries her face in my shoulder.

"I can't bear to look," she says with a sob.

But my eyes are glued to the scene before me as I hold her. All I see is my house, and I suddenly realize how deep Baba's and Mama's pain must be.

The women in the family wail and one of them collapses onto the road and sobs. An old man sits on the curb. His keffiyeh *flaps in the breeze over his crooked back. He leans his wrinkled hands on his knees as he tries to take in the scene before him. Even from across the road I can sense his desolation.*

Wooden frames, walls, steel pipes, kitchen cupboards, bathroom units, pieces of furniture, and blocks of cement lay strewn around the collapsing house. The bulldozer keeps going and we all cry out because there's nothing we can do. There's nothing we can do and we hate our helplessness.

"Is it over?" Maysaa asks.

"No," I whisper.

"Let's just leave."

I nod and we slowly start to walk away. Two army jeeps are parked at the edge of the street, the soldiers standing in front of them, guarding the demolition operation. Behind us, the crowd's chants rise higher, attracting more protestors. Some of the youths start to throw stones at the soldiers.

"We need to get out of here," I tell Maysaa.

"Quick!" she cries.

The soldiers fire rubber-coated bullets to disperse us. The single shots whistle past, lodging into the retaining walls of the houses behind us and smashing into the windows of the street's parked cars. Volleys of shots explode in the air. People scream; others pick up more stones from the road and hurl them at the soldiers. Bullets are sprayed in reply.

"Run!" we hear people cry. Maysaa and I sprint away from the scattering crowd, trying to find an alley to hide in

or a building to screen us. But one of the jeeps is chasing after the withdrawing crowd. We're about two hundred feet from the entrance to a side street, running alongside ten or twelve other kids and teenagers. The jeep, which is still chasing us, stops. One of the soldiers gets out. We make it to a building at the entrance of the street, but in our panic Maysaa and I trip over each other. "Yallah! Quick!" some-body shouts.

As we frantically collect ourselves off the ground, I look behind. The soldier is kneeling down. He takes aim and fires. The rubber bullets hit a window above us. I hear the jeep door close and the jeep skidding and speeding away. Then: excruciating pain. I have one clear thought: I want Mama. I turn to grab Maysaa's hand. But she's crumpled on the ground. A rubber bullet has shattered her forehead. I kneel down beside her, realizing that my face is oozing blood. Shards of glass from the window smashed by the bullet have hit me. My face is forever distorted with the shame of my clumsiness. I hold my hand up to my bleeding face, look at Maysaa, and vomit.

She died looking at me.

I'm suddenly being lifted from the ground. I force my eyes open and through blurred vision I see Yossi's face, grim and twisted with concentration as he carries me away. I turn my head and Samy is walking beside him.

The streets are quiet now. The protestors have dispersed. The soldiers are gone. Yossi carries me to his car and gently lays me on the backseat. Samy squeezes onto the floor space behind the passenger seat.

"We still have to get out of here unnoticed, given that you don't have the permit," Yossi cautions us. "Things will be even more tense after the protest. So stay down."

I'm disoriented and dizzy and exhausted and thirsty. I half prop myself up and my head swoons. "What happened?" I ask, lying back down.

Yossi lights a cigarette. He's sweating and uses the back of his arm to wipe his forehead.

"I couldn't drive away," he explains. "I was blocked. The police and army were everywhere. I waited in a nearby shop. I didn't want to be on the scene. Just in case things got nasty. When the crowd was breaking up and the police had rounded people up and were on their way, I returned to my car. That's when

I noticed Samy. He was walking around, calling your name."

"One minute you were next to me," Samy says, "and then you were gone."

"It was the tear gas. I couldn't see in front of me. And then, I don't know what happened, I panicked and sort of blacked out. I . . . everything came back to me and I lost control. . . ."

I'm worn out. I start to weep, covering my face with my shaking hands.

"Come on, Hayaat, stop crying," Samy says awkwardly. "It's OK, you're safe now."

"Maysaa . . . Sitti Zeynab . . ." I say between gasps of breath.

Yossi gives me a tissue. "Here, wipe your face. You'll be home soon. It will be OK."

I nod and blow my nose.

"I'll try and smuggle you out of Jerusalem," Yossi says gently. "I'll take you to Abu Dis. You can catch a service from there. It's safer than me trying to smuggle you through the Rachel's Tomb checkpoint in Bethlehem."

"Thanks," Samy says quietly.

"Can I call my parents?" I ask Yossi when I have the courage to speak without breaking down again.

He hits his hand on his head. "Of course! How silly of me." He hands me the phone.

"What's the time?" I ask him as I wait for somebody to pick up on the other end.

"Nearly eight."

Jihan answers.

"Hayaat? Oh my God! Where are you? Do you realize how worried we are? We called the school and there was no *dabka* practice today. Mama and Baba are having a fit here. Mama thinks you've been abducted! Have you been? Is there a ransom? Where are you?"

"I'm in . . . Jerusalem."

"*What?*"

I explain the situation to her. When I'm done she suddenly hollers, "Mama! She hasn't been abducted! Worse. She snuck into Jerusalem. And Samy's with her. They're with an Israeli."

I can hear Mama as clearly as if she were sitting next to me. "Al-Quds?! AL-QUDS? But how? What's going on? Give me the phone! Move! Quick! What do you

226

mean, 'snuck in'? Climbed the Wall? Foad, didn't I tell you that Samy boy was trouble? What girl thinks to climb the Wall? Now will you listen —"

"Hayaat, are you OK? Are you and Samy safe?"

Mama fires off a round of questions and I struggle to get a word in.

"Yossi? Who is this Yossi? An *Israeli?*"

Suddenly Baba is on the phone. "Can this Yossi man arrange to put you in a taxi to bring you home? Tell him we'll pay him whatever he wants. Let me speak to him."

I hand the phone to Yossi. "Can you speak to my father?"

He takes the phone from me and explains his plans to Baba. Baba must approve because I hear Yossi say, "It's no problem. I'm happy to do it."

Exhausted, I lie down again and close my eyes.

"Amto Christina is going to eat me alive," Samy mutters. "I'll probably be grounded for a year. She'll make me go to all her church meetings as punishment."

"We were so close, though. . . ."

"Yes . . . yes we were."

"All I can think of is how angry my parents are. . . . And how I've failed Sitti Zeynab."

"Don't be dumb. You tried. Look how far we got. Who would have thought?"

"But I didn't get her soil. How will she get better now?"

Yossi, who has finished talking to my father, looks at me in the rearview mirror. "What soil? What are you talking about?"

I tell him everything. He nods thoughtfully but doesn't say anything.

I desperately want to peek out the window and see Jerusalem as we leave it, but Yossi thinks it's safer to stay hidden as there's an increased police presence following the protest.

"Where are we now?" I ask Yossi after some time has passed.

"Just on the outskirts of Jerusalem," he says and suddenly pulls over to the side of the road.

"It may not be your grandmother's village," he says, pointing outside, "but it's Jerusalem." He leans over the passenger seat and hands me my backpack. I look at him and understand. I take out the hummus jar and step out of the car. Samy comes with me. In silence, we lean on our haunches on the side of the road and scoop the dirt and soil into the jar.

It's not Sitti Zeynab's village. But it's a little sprinkle of Jerusalem, and it will do.

EIGHTEEN

Yossi takes us to a taxi stand in Abu Dis. From there we catch a service to Bethlehem. It's almost midnight. I fall in and out of sleep, waking only when we approach a checkpoint and I have to produce my papers for the soldiers.

Relief floods through me when we arrive in Bethlehem. Driving through the familiar streets and alongside the long, gray concrete Wall, I know I'm home.

The driver agrees to take Samy and me directly to our street. We promise to pay him extra, but he says it's OK as our apartment building is on the way to his house.

The adults are hysterical. Mama is sobbing uncontrollably. She lunges forward and clasps me to her. Oblivious to the fact that Amto Christina and Amo

Joseph are fussing over Samy only footsteps away, Mama then launches into a tirade.

"Boys take risks!" she cries. "They like adventure. They think this is all a game. But you need to survive, not expose yourself to bad influences! See why I insist you play with girls? Are you OK? Have you been hurt? Oh, how could you put us through this? Thank God you're home!"

She doesn't let me explain. Trapped under her enormous bosom, my eyes meet Samy's. He's grinning, and I overhear Amto Christina and Amo Joseph scolding him, too, as they simultaneously shower him with kisses.

My heart lurches when Baba turns me toward him and places his hands on my shoulders. He looks me in the eyes and then, trying to stifle a sob, he hugs me tightly.

"You're safe," he says, over and over again. "You silly girl, you're safe."

Jihan comes running down the stairs of the apartment building and throws herself at me.

"I'm going to kill you!" she cries, hugging me tightly. "My wedding is only weeks away and you decide to go and risk your life. We're all stressed enough as it is! And did you take my treadmill money? I've been saving that money for ages!"

"I borrowed it," I say meekly.

"Oh, Jihan, be quiet," Mama says. "You really can be insensitive at times."

Baba laughs and Mama rolls her eyes at him.

"Where's Sitti Zeynab?" I finally ask as we walk up the stairs to our apartment.

"Frantic with worry," Mama says. "If a stroke nearly finished her off, can you imagine what your running away to Jerusalem did to her?"

"Oh, Nur, there's no need to exaggerate," Baba says. "Hayaat doesn't need to hear such things at a time like this. Sitti Zeynab is fine."

"Fine? She hasn't stopped praying since Tariq told her Hayaat had been kidnapped by *Mossad*!"

"Well, we sorted that story out, didn't we? And your mother is always praying. She'll calm down once she sees Hayaat."

My heart beats furiously as I open the door to our bedroom. Sitti Zeynab is propped against two navy blue pillows, reading from the Koran. She looks up and lets out a yelp. Her eyes are bright and untouched, having never caught up with the wrinkling, shrinking curse of the clock.

"Hayaat!" she cries and stretches her arms out to me. Entangled, her arms and my arms, her heartbeat and the sound of bullets firing in my brain, we cry. When we've caught our breath, she leans back against her pillows. And then, with shades of inflection — raspy, deep, smooth, and crackling — she sings for me.

> *The breeze of our homeland revives the body*
> *And surely we cannot live without our homeland*
> *The bird cries when it is thrown out of its nest*
> *So how is the homeland that has its own people?*

Her face is stern as her voice quivers with both melancholy and delight. Her eyebrows are knitted and the palms of her hands raised up as if in prayer.

When she's finished she smiles. "Oh, how happy I am to see you!" she says. "Perhaps now I'll have some peace and quiet. Your mother has been driving me crazy, fussing over me as though I were a sick old lady." She grins at me. "Do me a favor, *habibti*. Don't let your mother feed me any more of her vegetable soup. God knows she's a good cook, but I can't bear to taste another cabbage leaf. Does she think some stinking cabbage broth is going to change God's plans for me?"

"And it can't help your digestion," I add with a smile, making a mental note to sleep with the windows open tonight.

"Tell me, Hayaat," she says. "Tell me you're OK."

"I was so scared, Sitti," I say in a quiet voice. "Ever since the day Maysaa died, I've choked on my memories. She's been wrapped around my neck. All I've wanted is for my mind to fall asleep. And then, when we were in Jerusalem — "

"You made it there . . . ?"

"Yes," I say. "We made it. But the timing was all wrong. We got caught in a protest. And that's when I remembered everything. It all came flooding back to me. . . . I miss Maysaa so much. . . . And I feel so guilty because I miss her but I can't help but think about my face too. Yet how can I think about that when she's lying in the ground and I'm still alive? I'm so weak." I smear my dripping nose on my arm.

"*Nur ayni*, light of my eyes," Sitti Zeynab says, wheezing slightly. "How can you call yourself weak? You? *Weak?* Your soul is strong, Hayaat. Do not deprive the world of your soul and heart. Justice will come when those who hope outweigh those who despair. Hope is a force that cannot be reckoned with, *ya* Hayaat. You will find a place for yourself in this world. Ignore the fat aunties and uncles who pity you because of your scars. I don't pity you. I look up to you. But, Hayaat, why would you dare to enter Jerusalem?"

I sit up and give her a sober look. "I want you to know that I tried, Sitti," I say. "And Samy too."

"I don't understand. Tried what?"

"To reach your village. To bring you back some soil . . . We made it to the wall of the Old City. It was just as you described it."

"Oh God!" she moans. "You mean you went because of me?"

"Well, yes."

"Never listen to the ramblings of an old woman, Hayaat! Between you and me I don't even know what day it is today. How could you possibly rely on anything I've said to undertake such a crazy journey? It is my burden to bear, putting such an idea in your head."

"My head is my own, Sitti. It was my idea."

"I planted the seed. I'm still responsible. I am a fool. I have one foot in the grave and I still have a severed soul, one half in my village, one half here. Even though my head tells me I will die in this house, in this town, I must confess to you, Hayaat, that my heart whispers treacherous promises: *You will return*, it tells me. It does not do to cling to false hope. But it does not do to live without it either. . . . Oh, there I go again. I need to stop talking."

She sinks her head into the pillows. Her scarce, light eyelashes flutter down for a moment. "Is it precious because it was taken from us or was it precious to begin with?" she asks, her eyes still shut.

"It shouldn't matter," I say. I jump out of the bed and place the backpack on the bed between us.

She opens her eyes. "What's this?"

I unzip the bag and produce the hummus jar.

"I've already eaten, *habibti*, thank you."

I quickly open the jar and thrust it into her hands. "Look," I say.

Frowning, she peers into the jar. She takes a sharp breath.

I take the jar from her. "Open your hands." I pour some soil into her open palms. "Jerusalem soil," I whisper.

I see her eyes and I know that every step of our journey was worth this moment.

With the wedding only a month away, Mama and Jihan intend to keep me busy after school. Jihan picks me up from the school gates, producing her hot pink notebook and matching pen with white tulle flowing from one end. Glancing at her to-do list, her lips pouted in concentration, she excitedly reveals the afternoon's chore. Today we're shopping for wedding shoes, and I'm forced to watch her and Mama argue about shades of white. At one point I'm invited to give my opinion.

"This one or that one?" Jihan asks, holding up two identical pairs of white shoes.

"Um . . . what's the difference?"

"Well, do you prefer this white or that white?" she asks impatiently.

"Say the left," Mama hisses at me.

Bewildered, I tell them I have a headache and run off and wait for them at the counter.

This evening a curfew of eight hours is imposed. There have been clashes near Rachel's Tomb when bull-dozers started on some of the shops and surrounding houses that are in the path of the Wall. Mama is furious. She had invited some of her friends for dinner tonight. Baba is also angry, although his feelings are somewhat placated by the fact that he'll be able to stay at home (he'd planned to escape Mama's friends by playing cards at Amo Hisham's house) and treat himself to all the special delicacies Mama has painstakingly prepared.

We sit in the living room, sharing a communion of solemn silence as we listen to Mama from the kitchen. Tariq sits on Jihan's lap, his eyes wide open with both curiosity and fear. Baba has not dared enter the kitchen to burn his *argeela* coal over the stove and has resorted to Mama's packet of cigarettes. Even Mohammed has fallen asleep earlier than usual.

Although Sitti Zeynab is not well, her energy for talking has not been sapped, but she, too, is exercising uncommon restraint, keeping her Koranic verses, Prophet's sayings, and Arabic proverbs to a bare minimum and only just under her breath.

"All that meat and chicken!" Mama grumbles. "Do they think I wake up and find money under my pillow?" The lid of a pot bangs down. "The first time I invite them over and" — the fridge door slams shut — "the *knafa* was perfect! Let them even try to clot the cream with honey the way I do." A pot is thumped down onto the kitchen bench. "And that blithering fool, Sarah, tells me not to worry" — a cabinet door crashes closed — "we can reschedule and have it at her place. How" — *thwack* — "dare" — *thud* — "she" — *slam* — "miss the point?"

Then the phone rings. "I'll get it," Mama hollers. "It must be Yosra." She plunges into the living room, her eyes daring us to contradict her.

"Yes? OK . . . yes . . . of course . . . yes, we will make noise too."

Discreetly, we exchange raised eyebrows and wait for Mama to finish.

She sighs deeply, runs her fingers through her hair, which Jihan had blow-dried and styled, and then wipes her lipstick onto the back of her hand.

"There's to be a demonstration," she says. "Jihan, Hayaat, go get the pots, pans, and ladles. Foad, open all the windows."

It's a case of Abu Somebody, telephoning Um Anybody, who tells Abu Everybody that at midnight everyone should bang on their pots and pans in protest at the curfew.

Tariq, Jihan, and I grab on to metal ladles and pound down hard on Mama's pots and pans, positioning ourselves in front of the windows of our apartment, competing with the drumming sounds emanating from nearby homes. Sweat trickles down our faces, our cheeks redden with the effort, and we squeal in delight as our house comes alive with the crashing and echoing sounds of our protest. Mohammed, who has inevitably woken, sits in Sitti Zeynab's lap, his bobbing head following the sounds. Sitti Zeynab looks at us and laughs. "Louder! Louder!" she cries, egging us on. Even Mama and Baba join in. I've never seen Mama so animated. The pot she is banging on is dented by the time she's finished. Her hair is matted with sweat, her eyes are almost insane with glee as she smashes the Tefal nonstick pan. Baba has to hold her back when she lunges for another.

"We need at least one pan left to roast a chicken in," he says.

Samy approaches me moments before the school bell rings for lunch, wanting to know if I'll skip school to join him. He's going to church.

"What? You mean voluntarily?"

"Yeah."

"OK. I guess I owe you a visit anyway."

He leads me to the Church of Nativity. When we arrive I follow him through a corridor of massive archways made of chiseled brown and beige stone. I've never been so deep inside the church. Not because I'm Muslim, but because at my age, churches, mosques, schools, and the dentist's office are normally places to avoid.

We enter two huge doors and step inside. Candles throw giant shadows on the ancient walls. The heavy incense tickles my nose and makes me dizzy. Rows and rows of enormous marble pillars line the open space and lead to another massive double door. The floor is marble of different shades of gray and white. We walk to the altar and I'm stunned by the richness of the church. The place is filled with gold and silver, cascading chandeliers and candelabras.

"Wow," I whisper. "It's beautiful."

"Follow me," Samy says quietly.

"Where are we going?"

"The Grotto."

"What's that?"

"Where Jesus was born, stupid. Everyone knows that."

"What are we going to do there? I'm Muslim, remember."

"Yes, I know that! I want to light a candle."

"Why?"

"For my father," he says, without looking at me. "It's seven years today."

"Oh." I feel ashamed to have forgotten.

We descend a flight of stairs to an oblong-shaped altar.

Tourists and worshippers are gathered around a silver star fitted into the white marble paving.

"How could they fit a bed in here?" I whisper to Samy. "Or did Mary give birth on that stone floor?"

Samy gives me an exasperated look. "She gave birth in a stable. And this was later built over it. Don't they teach Muslims *anything*?"

"I don't even listen in my own religion classes, let alone yours."

He nods solemnly. "Fair enough."

He lights a candle and approaches the silver star.

"Can I light one for your father too?" I whisper hesitantly.

He passes me a candle and nods. We lean down next to each other and pray.

On our way home Samy asks me if I'm ready.

I look at him blankly. "Ready for what?"

"To find Wasim. Don't you wonder if he waited for me? At the pharmacy?"

"Oh . . . yes! I forgot all about him."

"Typical girl. This is soccer we're talking about,

Hayaat! I want to find him. I'm going to Aida camp tomorrow. After school. We can say we have *dabka* practice."

I raise an eyebrow at him.

"OK, we'll try another excuse. Shoot, we'll never be able to use *dabka* practice again. You're coming, yes?"

"Sure. But I can't tomorrow. Jihan wants me to help her pack her bags."

"Why?"

This time I raise both eyebrows.

He gives me a sheepish look. "Oh yeah. The wedding . . . Well, we'll go the day after tomorrow."

"OK."

"It's going to happen, Hayaat," he says excitedly, rubbing his hands together. "I'm sure to impress the coach. And then watch me leave this place! Watch me become a huge star. And then I'll buy my way back here and I'll find somebody to pay so I can see my father. Money talks, Hayaat. Just think of what my father will say!"

NINETEEN

Sitti Zeynab is tired. She asks me to help her to her bed. She leans her heavy body against me and I slowly lead her to the bedroom. I help her get comfortable and pull the blanket up to her chest, fluffing the pillows behind her. Her white veil is draped around her head; wisps of her hair fall across her face. Her breathing is labored and her breath stale.

"My life has been all politics," she whispers as she touches the pile of photographs of my aunts and uncles on her bedside table. "I do not watch the television for politics because it is in every breath I take. It is here in this apartment, in the empty chairs that should hold my children who were forced to scatter around the world. It is here in the mint leaves floating in this cup of tea beside my bed. Mint leaves that should have been picked from the flower bed in my home, not bought from Abu Yusuf's store. It is in the olives I eat from somebody else's tree and the patch of sky I am told I must live under."

I pat her hand. "Calm down, Sitti. You need to save your energy. Don't work yourself up."

She reaches a hand out and touches my face.

"Hayaat, I have sometimes wanted a refund on my dreams. I have known feelings of such desolation that they have threatened to bury me under the ground. I have sobbed for my land and it cries out for me in return. But I have watched you grow, Jihan fall in love, Mohammed arrive into this world, Tariq enter school. My heart, it is like a flower and you are like my petals. What more do I need?" She kisses the top of my head. "Now, be a good girl and bring me my medicine."

"It's with Mama."

"She thinks I'm too senile to know what to take. Pah! My body may be giving up on me but my mind is still sharp, Hayaat. And anyway, she's the one who spent an hour looking for her purse yesterday. It was in her sock drawer. Did she tell you that?"

I shake my head and smile. When I pass by the bedroom a little later, I peek in. Sitti Zeynab is asleep, snoring loudly. Her hands are resting on her chest, her fingers barely touching the jar of soil, which she must have reached across to her bedside table to get.

I absorb her face like it's the last kite of summer and grin from ear to ear.

"So next week, we'll pick up my dress. Can you believe it, Hayaat? It's all happening so soon. Ahmad's mother keeps calling me. Tells me she can't wait for the wedding. She seems nice. I just hope she's not one of those interfering witches. Well, she hasn't interfered in any of our decisions yet. Huh! Maybe Ahmad will be the one with the problems with Mama. . . ."

I sit on Sitti Zeynab's bed, helping Jihan sort the clothes she's taking with her and the clothes she's leaving for me.

"Here, you can have this dress," Jihan says, tossing it to me.

"Thanks!" I exclaim, running my hands over the silk fabric. "Are you sure, though? You'll have lots of weddings and parties to go to when you're a bride."

"Ah, don't worry about it. It's too small for me anyway."

Sitti Zeynab hobbles into the room and takes a seat on the edge of her bed. "What are you doing?" she asks Jihan.

"Sorting out my clothes, Sitti."

"May God protect you. May you know happiness. May your new family treat you with love and kindness. May we see you often. Oh God, may we see you often. And may you have many babies."

"*Ameen*," Jihan murmurs automatically.

"God bless your mother-in-law and father-in-law and their brothers and their sisters and —"

I shoot Jihan a panicked look. "Quick," I hiss, "this could go on for hours!"

"Will you miss me, Sitti Zeynab?" Jihan interrupts, flopping down next to Sitti Zeynab. She slings an arm over Sitti Zeynab's frail shoulders and gives her an affectionate squeeze. "Who will give you trouble when I'm gone? Oh, this house will be empty without me!"

Sitti Zeynab breaks out into silent laughter, her shoulders jiggling up and down.

"Don't worry, Sitti. Hayaat will be here. She's your favorite anyway. Traveling to Jerusalem on her own for a jar of soil. *I'd* never do that." Jihan winks at me and I poke my tongue out at her.

"God help your in-laws," Sitti Zeynab says, making Jihan giggle.

"What's the joke?" Mama asks as she walks in. Without waiting for an answer she continues talking. "Jihan, don't take *everything* with you. You don't even wear half your clothes. Have you packed all your new clothes? Oh, please don't take that awful pair of jeans. They're frayed at the bottom! And don't tell me it's the fashion!"

"But it is!"

"Hayaat, take them out of the suitcase. I won't have my daughter entering her new home with ripped clothes. What would your mother-in-law say? I'll tell you what she'd say. She'd say: 'What kind of mother brought you up to wear torn clothes?' She'd say —"

"Oh, Mama," Jihan scoffs.

Jihan skips over to the CD player and turns on the music. She dances around Mama, grabbing my hand and pulling me up with her. Tariq runs into the room and imitates our dancing, poking fun at us and making funny faces.

"I'm getting married," Jihan sings. Sitti Zeynab claps to the music. Mama starts to wail. Baba runs in and cries: "What's wrong? What's happened?"

"She's leaving us for Ramallah," Mama howls.

"*Ya habibti*," Sitti croaks. "That is life. Think how many children I have said good-bye to. First there was Saleem —"

Jihan throws her arms around Mama and laughs.

"Oh, Mama, it will be fine. I'll make you a grandmother one day! Huh! How funny! What a young *sito* you will be."

Baba, embarrassed by the display of emotions, smiles shyly and then withdraws quietly.

Jihan skips around us. "Ahmad says we're going to dance all night. And, Hayaat, you'll be the best *dabka* dancer there! Ahmad's hired a brilliant band!"

Mama makes Jihan promise that she'll call every day and consult only her for recipes. "Do that for me, Jihan," Mama says. "Don't ask Ahmad's mother. Ask *me*."

That night I turn over in bed and notice Jihan lying wide-awake, staring at the ceiling.

"Can't you sleep?" I whisper.

She shakes her head.

"What's wrong?"

Her face seems to collapse then and she half giggles, half chokes.

"Did you fight with Ahmad?"

Sniffling, she shakes her head. I creep out of bed, find a tissue box, and return, handing it to her. As quietly as possible, she blows her nose and wipes her eyes. We lie side by side, our heads facing each other on the same pillow.

"It just occurred to me. That's all."

"What?"

"What if Ahmad and I end up bickering all the time? Like Mama and Baba? And what if he's messy and expects me to clean up after him?"

"Oh, that's OK. You're messy anyway so what's the problem?"

She thinks for a moment and then smiles. "Yes, I'm messy. . . . Oh God!" Her eyes widen. "What if he's neat?"

"He can clean up after you."

"Ha! Yeah, right, he would!" She muffles her laughter into the pillow. Then she looks at me with wide eyes. "Oh God. What if I need to, you know, go to the bathroom or fart?" She giggles. "How embarrassing, Hayaat. Oh, I couldn't. I'll never go to the bathroom again."

"Don't be silly. Mama and Baba fart in front of each other all the time and they're still married."

"I love him, Hayaat. Here, read this text he sent me this evening." She reaches under her pillow for her phone and shows me the message. You dance barefoot at the entrance to my heart.

"Did he make that up?"

"No. It's a song. It's all about the application."

"Oh. Nice."

We lie there in silence for a few moments.

"Yes, I love him. But . . ." A tear rolls down her face and she wipes it away. "How stupid I am, crying like a child. . . . I'm going to miss you all."

"We won't miss you. We'll have more room in the bed now. And longer shower time. And —"

"You brat," she says, hitting me on the arm.

"Do you think anybody will ever love me?" I ask after a long pause.

"Of course!"

"Shh. You'll wake Sitti Zeynab."

"Of course," she repeats in a hushed tone. "Why on earth . . ."

I raise my hand to my face, tracing the scars. "I'm like a shattered glass pane," I murmur. "Even when you put the glass back together, the cracks still show."

She grabs my chin in her hand and forces me to look her in the eye. "You're beautiful, you silly thing. I couldn't have survived a second. . . ." Her voice falters and I look away, swallowing the sudden lump in my throat. "I look up to you, Hayaat. I'm an ungrateful wretch of a girl and sometimes I wonder what Ahmad sees in me." A moment of silence passes between us, then she casually adds: "The poor guy, he doesn't know what he's in for."

We giggle and, when we catch our breath, I snuggle into her chest and close my eyes. I'm tired of words. At that moment it's enough for me to sleep dreamlessly in my sister's arms.

TWENTY

Mama asks me to keep her company while she rolls the grape leaves for the next day's evening meal. I watch her spoon the raw rice, tomato, and parsley into the grape leaves spread out on the small table. The kitchen is tiny compared to the cavernous space we had in our home in Beit Sahour. Our kitchen there had a double door that opened onto a balcony overlooking an orchard filled with orange and lemon trees. In the middle of the room was a beechwood oval table that sat eight people. On one wall was a long buffet for Mama's dinner sets and crockery. The kitchen in the apartment reminds me of a closet. Small and stuffy, it can't even fit the freezer, which has to be kept at the end of the hallway.

"I was angry with you for going to Jerusalem," Mama says, her voice uncharacteristically low. "How I worried when you didn't come home from school that day. You must promise never to do such a thing again."

"Yes, Mama," I mutter automatically.

"It was very brave, Hayaat. . . ."

Surprised by her compliment, I look up into her eyes and she smiles.

"But it was still foolish."

"Yes, Mama."

"Here, take a spoon and help me. You'll have your own house one day, but you will only ever have one kitchen to learn from. For the sake of my heart, I pray you choose a boy from here. Or from Beit Sahour, our real hometown. Although it would be better he lived here, now that we're here. Don't overstuff the leaves, *habibti*, or they will be hard to roll. The smaller they are, the better the compliments. So tell me, Hayaat. Did you see the Old City? Was it as beautiful as they say?"

"Yes. But Mama . . . it isn't Beit Sahour."

"Ahh, Beit Sahour," she says and smiles. "You were only nine when we came here. Were you too young to remember how good the hills smelled? The open landscape? I enjoyed breathing there. . . ." She glances at me. "You know, Hayaat, sometimes the past is so tangible I feel as though I can grab the memories with my hands, bring them up to my face, and taste them." She leans toward me. "Do you remember the day they came for our land?"

I nod and she continues. Her words, which usually run out of her mouth, decide to stroll this time, and I'm glad for the unusual calmness in her voice.

"We were given a confiscation order. They were going to build a road to connect the settlements to each other. . . . Your father came home from the field. I handed him the order. . . . He tore it up and we sat down to eat. He refused to speak about it that night.

"We lived in fear for two years, Hayaat, wondering when the bulldozers would arrive." Her voice falters and her heavily kohled eyes fix on the grape leaf she's been rolling.

"Mama . . . ?"

I'm not accustomed to seeing Mama like this. She's always had a no-nonsense approach to emotions. Unlike Baba, who I've regularly seen locked in his own reverie, Mama seems too busy to reflect on anything except managing the house and looking after us.

She contrives a smile and lets out a weary sigh. "I'm OK, Hayaat. I'm just surprised at how vivid my memories of those days are."

"I remember one day you told us we had to empty the house of everything and Jihan and I were arguing about who owned which toys."

"That was when we got the demolition notice — put more rice in that one, Hayaat — we had a week to move out. Some of our neighbors also had demolition notices. We were all in a state of panic, Hayaat, vying for first access to the few moving vans in town. . . ." She chuckles and shakes her head. "I had a big fight with Um Tamer about it. She had one living room and two bedrooms. We had one living room, one family room, veranda furniture, two dining-table sets, and *four* bedrooms. And she wanted the bigger van. . . . I never liked that woman. She moved in with her daughter and son-in-law. Still, I feel sorry for her. She doesn't get along with her son-in-law. Although I don't blame him. . . ."

"Mama, the day they came . . . why did you send Sitti Zeynab, Jihan, and me away to town with Khalto Aneesa? Khalto Aneesa bought us lunch. I remember that. I also remember Jihan was in a foul mood. She said you were treating her like a child."

"She wouldn't forgive me when you returned and there was nothing left. But I didn't want you all to see.

"First they destroyed the water tanks, the ones we used to irrigate the farmland. Then a building your father used to store agricultural equipment. Your father . . . well, you have never seen him in such a state and it's unlikely you ever will. . . .

"The worst part was how noisy the demolition was, and how slow. When they came for our house I lost control of myself, Hayaat. I ran toward it but a line of soldiers was barricading the front gate, protecting the bulldozers. I wanted to hit them. I wanted to crush them. I've never felt such rage. The walls fell and I broke."

"And Baba?"

"The neighbors had to hold him back. They pinned him down onto the ground as he screamed. . . . They started on the trees" — her voice becomes a whisper — "and it was the most terrible thing of all."

"I miss our land. Mama, it's all under concrete now. The orchard. The house. I think of the cars that drive on the road and . . . I wonder if they don't know or don't care."

She leans back in her chair and gazes wistfully at me. Then she smiles, her eyes crinkly and sweet. "We have two choices in this world," she says in a matter-of-fact tone. "We either try to survive or we give up."

TWENTY-ONE

We slip out of school an hour early.

"I'll race you to the camp!"

I shoot after Samy, happy to feel my feet pound against the ground and make my heart and lungs dance inside me. When we arrive at Aida, my eyes take in the sharp difference between the camp and the town. Since moving from Beit Sahour to Bethlehem, I have become accustomed to the belfries, towers, domes, and church steeples. But in Aida the dwellings are a tight grid of concrete-block apartment buildings with heavy steel doors separated by very narrow alleys. Bullet holes decorate some of the graffiti-covered walls. There are people everywhere, packed on top of each other like colored lentils in a jar. There are malnourished children our age and younger, with dark circles under their eyes, torn clothes sitting baggily on their thin frames, playing in the litter-strewn streets and alleys. But there are also children dressed in neat school uniforms, juggling piles of books and heavy backpacks. I walk through the camp, finding it hard to picture it when it was a collection of tents and Sitti Zeynab and Sidi Yusuf sat within four poles with my uncles, aunts, and mother at their feet. There is an enduring quality to the camp; the matrix of solid buildings seems starkly permanent. Posters of people killed by the occupation are on poles and in shop windows. Posters with men, women, children, and babies stare at me, frozen in time. They are part of the camp's permanence and yet, I realize, it's the struggle against such permanence that killed them.

We approach a man standing outside a mixed goods store. Samy, who has memorized Wasim's address, asks the man for directions.

"Do you think he would have forgotten to speak to the coach?" Samy asks me as we follow the man's instructions.

"I pity him if he did!" I joke, but Samy's face creases with worry lines. We pass a butcher and my stomach turns at the sight of the sheep and cows stripped of their skin swinging in the shopfront. How funny that I forget such repulsion as soon as I sit down to a steaming plate of Mama's *maklobe*.

Samy's creased face suddenly smooths out and, in a buoyant tone, he says: "I'm sure he remembered! How could he forget with me pestering him like I did? I told the guys at school, you know. They're so envious."

"Huh!" I grunt. "Why do boys all like to compete with each other?"

Samy gives me a strange look.

We soon find the street on which Wasim lives. His uncle sits in front of their apartment building, an *argeela* pipe resting in his mouth. However, I notice there's no coal on the foil covering the tobacco. He studies us as we approach him and then bursts into strange hysterical laughter. Frightened, I take a step backward, but Samy stays put. Suddenly the door bursts open and a woman rushes out. "Mo'ayad!" she cries, wrapping her arms around his shoulders to calm him.

"What do you want?" she asks us.

Speechless, I can only stare at her.

"We're looking for Wasim," Samy says.

"He's playing soccer with his friends."

Samy flashes me a conspiratorial grin and asks her for directions.

"I wonder what's wrong with him," I say as we walk to a nearby alleyway where Wasim is apparently playing.

"He seems harmless. . . ."

Wasim is alone. A soccer ball lies on the ground beside him. He's bending down, pulling his socks up; when he hears the shuffle of our feet, he looks up and sees us.

"You came!" he exclaims, grinning with delight and quickly rising. "I waited for you at the pharmacy every day this week, *ya zalami*! We were going to play soccer. Remember?"

Samy marches up to him. "Did you speak to the coach?" he asks anxiously.

Wasim's eyes instantly give him away. Flustered, he wrings his hands together, looking down at the ground and then back up.

"I . . . of course it wasn't true, *ya zalami*. I mean, they were thinking of a team, the people who came here from overseas to help us, but, well, I was joking. It was just a bit of fun. I thought you would work it out. It's all about the soccer, though, isn't it? I mean, I'm an excellent player, I assure you. There *was* an *Englizee* coach once. He was here as a volunteer. He did tell me I was *momtaz*. I promise. Look, we could have a really brilliant match. And you could bring some of your other friends. Yes?"

"You swore you were telling the truth!" I say. "On your mother's grave, you said."

"My mother's not dead," Wasim says matter-of-factly.

I stamp a foot on the ground in frustration. "We believed you. Crooked buildings and . . . and . . . knee pads!"

Wasim flashes a lopsided guilty grin.

"Why did you lie?" I press.

"I don't know," he mutters.

Samy is silent. A nauseating tension seeps through the alley. Wasim's words and mine are like lightning flashes inviting the crack of thunder.

"I was . . . bored. . . ." Wasim offers. I realize his eyes are incapable of masking his loneliness.

"Talk, talk, talk!" Samy cries and lunges at Wasim,

pushing him to the ground and pinning him down as he straddles him.

Wasim starts to cry. "I'm sorry!" he manages through his tears.

"You're a liar!" Samy yells hysterically. "You made me believe I could get out of this dump! You liar!"

I've never seen Samy lose control like this and suddenly I'm afraid.

"I'm sorry!" Wasim cries out again. Snot is dribbling down onto his mouth and I gag.

"Get off him, Samy," I say, trying to sound composed.

Samy raises his fist, ready to punch Wasim. "I'm going to beat the crap out of him!" he yells.

"Samy! No!"

"Stay out of this, Hayaat!"

"Get off me!" Wasim screams.

I grab Samy's arm and pull him away. "Samy, stop! Have you gone crazy?"

Our eyes lock. For a second I hardly recognize him. Then his face collapses and he falls to the side of Wasim, who's sobbing loudly.

"Shut up!" Samy yells at Wasim.

"Don't hurt me!" Wasim cries, raising his hands to his face.

Samy gives us both a disgusted look and then takes off, sprinting out of the alley.

"Wait!" I cry and chase after him.

The camp is full of alleyways and passages, and my heart pounds hard as I try to match Samy's cracking pace and keep him in sight.

"Stop!" I cry out, panting, but he doesn't. I follow him through the crowded streets, dodging pedestrians and traffic. My lungs are burning now and I want to cry from the pain. Finally, Samy turns into a dingy alley between two crumbling apartment buildings. It's a dead end. Parked at the end is a wrecked car. The alley reeks; overflowing garbage bags lie in stinking piles here and there.

I stop and rest my hands on my knees, leaning forward and trying to catch my breath. I'm too shattered to look at Samy. I concentrate on relaxing my lungs. I wonder where Wasim is but then I decide I don't care. I don't care about anything except breathing.

Finally my lungs calm and that's when I hear the sound of glass smashing. I look up and see Samy standing next to the car. Shards of glass dangle precariously from the rear window. The backseat of the car is covered in shattered glass. Samy bobs down to the ground and picks up a big rock.

"Stop!" I yell. I run up to him. I'm angry now. Angry that he's lost control. Angry that things have turned out this way. Angry at Wasim, at this stinking alley, at stupid soccer dreams. But most of all I'm angry at Samy for giving up so easily.

I place myself between him and the car and give him a menacing look. "Put that down," I say in a no-nonsense tone. "Get a grip. You're acting like someone who's escaped from an asylum."

"Mind your own business. You're always in my face."

"Yeah, and that's a good thing. Somebody with a bit of sense has to keep an eye on you."

"This has nothing to do with you."

"I'm not going anywhere," I say, folding my arms across my chest. "You've already damaged this car and nearly bashed Wasim. And I bet you still feel like crap."

"Yeah, I do. But I'd feel better if you shut up and let me smash this other window."

He moves to the front of the car and raises the rock, aiming it at the windshield. "Get out of the way or you'll get hurt."

"You moron, look at my face. There's glass lodged in there that the doctors couldn't even remove. You think I'm scared of a bit of windshield? Go ahead." I'm scared but I stand my ground, trying to sound as fearless as I can.

Samy seems determined. He raises the rock higher and I resist taking a step back. He takes aim again and then screams, throwing the rock against the wall, away from us. He falls to the ground and starts to cry noiselessly. I'm shocked. It's too terrible to imagine Samy crying, let alone witness it.

I don't approach him until he regains control.

He scrunches his knees up under his chin and stares down at the ground. I take a tentative step toward him, slowly lower myself down to his level, and then sit down.

"If you tell anyone I cried —"

"Cried?" I scoff, cutting him off. "I didn't see you cry."

He nods once.

We sit for a while. I stare at the broken glass on the ground. The last rays of the afternoon sun bounce off the little pieces and create small rainbows on the wall.

It's Samy who breaks the silence. "I told you there was no point in dreaming."

"That's not true. . . . It's all we have. Sitti Zeynab says —"

He looks up, his face twisted with disappointment and anger.

"You have a grandmother to talk to, but my mother is dead and my father is locked up. I can't speak to Amto Christina and Amo Joseph. I've got nobody. . . . I'm nobody. I thought this would be my chance. . . . Well, there's no point, is there?"

"There is a point. . . . Look at me. My face is wrecked. And Maysaa is dead. Samy, she's dead! And Baba mopes around all day and Mama nags and Sitti Zeynab remembers and always there's the mirror or reflection in a shop window, reminding me of that day. But Mama says we have two choices in this world. We either try to survive or we give up."

"But I don't want to simply survive. Can't you see the difference between surviving and living?"

"I don't know. . . . There are times I want to curl up in my bed and shut down. . . . But I think . . . well, I think it's easier to hope than to give up. It doesn't seem that way but it is. I look at Baba and his depression is eating away at him. But I look at Sitti Zeynab. And she can still laugh and forgive."

"Forgive?" he says bitterly. "Never."

I shrug. "Who knows? But maybe Mama's wrong, Samy."

"What do you mean?"

"Maybe it's not about survival. Maybe we have to learn how to live with purpose."

"Well, what's my purpose?"

"How am I supposed to know?"

"You mentioned it."

"All I know is that it's not contained in this alley. And it was never in Wasim's hands."

He stands up and dusts off his trousers. "What's that smell?"

I stand up too. "It's the alley. Of all the places to stop in, you had to choose this dump."

"It's not my camp. How was I supposed to know where to stop? I was tired. An empty alley seemed like a good idea at the time."

"Leave the good ideas to me next time."

"You sure do talk a lot."

I raise an eyebrow at him. "What did you expect? That I'd let you break Wasim's nose?"

"At least it would have felt good and we could have avoided all this girl talk."

I throw my hands in the air. "I give up on you!"

"Don't do that, Hayaat," he says quietly. "Come on, I'll race you back."

TWENTY-TWO

I ask Baba to take me to visit Maysaa's grave. I haven't been since the funeral and I want to say good-bye properly. He's surprised but he agrees.

He walks with me through the Christian quarter of the cemetery. I grab on to his hand. He squeezes it tightly and I'm glad.

"Here it is," Baba says softly, and I look at the headstone. Fresh flowers have been placed against the stone. I bury my face against Baba.

"It's OK," he says quietly, over and over again. "She's at peace. To God do we belong and to God will we return, Hayaat." I remember hearing that when Maysaa's mother returned home from the funeral, she closed the bedroom door behind her, sat in front of her dressing table, and tore out chunks of her hair with her fingers. Plucked it out like a cook plucking the feathers from a chicken. She wore a black veil to the funeral. Her husband and sons held her up as she wailed and beat her fists on her chest.

My face was covered in bandages. People stared at me, and I wanted to climb into Maysaa's coffin and bury myself with her. Mama held me tight, ensconcing me against her soft stomach as tears poured down her face. Baba wore his *keffiyeh* and carried a pocket-sized Koran in his trembling hands. He didn't read from it, merely stroked its edges, turning it over and over in his hands. He didn't bring his larger Koran. Maysaa was Christian and Baba didn't want to offend her family, although, as all good Muslims do, he probably prayed for her soul and, as all good Christians do, they probably prayed for ours.

The coffin was mahogany; the priest's face rosy pink. He stood over the coffin, reading aloud from the Bible. Maysaa's brothers threw themselves onto the coffin, their eyes wild with grief as they hugged and kissed the wood. I wanted to run up to them and reassure them Maysaa was not, could not be, lying lifeless in that box of wood. Later that night I marveled at the fact that the moon rose and the stars shone as though untouched by Maysaa's death. *They had no right*, I thought to myself.

As I watched Maysaa's coffin being lowered into the ground, I tried to ignore people's stares and hushed conversations about me. The priest was talking about Maysaa returning to the Creator. He was telling us to be brave. He didn't understand that she was going to be a *dabka* star. That we had dreams about winning every competition. That we planned to make it to the championships and maybe even get on TV. Nobody understood that she died with her eyes open because she wasn't ready to leave.

I hid behind my bandages, fighting back the tears. I watched them bury Maysaa and I wanted to vomit. I kept seeing her bullet-shattered head, her lifeless body. The men poured dirt over the coffin and I willed myself to throw my memories of that day into the hole in the ground.

But instead my memories of all the good times with Maysaa had been buried.

"Hayaat?" Baba cups my chin in his hand and tilts my head up. "You'll be OK. I know. You're stronger than I am. Sometimes I feel like I've failed you all. I cling to the past when I know it's dangerous to do so. . . . But if I let go, what else do I have?"

"You have us."

"Yes, I know, and whether in Beit Sahour or Bethlehem, you are my world. But on my land I was able to give you more, and they took that from me. I wish I had your courage, Hayaat."

"Me?"

He nods. "You're not crushed by your memories the way I am."

Oh, but I was, I want to tell him. And yet, since Jerusalem, my memories of that day have beaten their fists against a door in my head. But finally, wonderfully, I'm able to refuse them entrance.

It's strange, but I feel calm and in control. I've walked through that day too many times. On the streets of Jerusalem I relived it and in fact I'm now glad to have faced that day head-on. Because there were so many days with Maysaa before that day and there are so many days without her ahead of me. And I'm beginning to understand that the haunting will stop when I remember Maysaa not as a ghost but as the second-best *dabka* dancer in class, who always chewed gum, pulled her socks up to her knees, and drank her daily can of Pepsi with two straws.

Baba takes my hand. "Are you ready to say good-bye to Maysaa now?"

"No," I say with a smile. "Never."

It's the week before the wedding. Mama trains us to be robotic cleaning machines. We wash the walls, polish the furniture, color-code the linen closet, scrub the stainless-steel pots until they're like mirrors, dust the shelves and photo frames, change the linens, and mop the floors. Baba and Mama rearrange the furniture, trying to maximize the space in preparation for Ahmad, who's coming to pick up Jihan to take her to the wedding reception in Ramallah. His family and friends, depending on who can pass through the checkpoints, are also accompanying him.

"But they're not even going to stay!" I groan. "They're coming to pick her up and then leave! So what's the point?"

"People will visit. Now clean!" Mama bellows.

I scowl at her and take the pile of towels and throw it into the closet, hoping it'll make an angry thud on the shelf.

Khalo Hany, who lives in Jordan, has been refused a permit to enter. It's too expensive for Khalto Ibtisam, who lives in America, and Khalo Sharif, who lives in Australia, to bring their families, and they have work commitments anyway. Sitti Zeynab understands their situation but is still disappointed.

"It's the first wedding for us here. If it's too expensive for the whole family, why can't Ibtisam and Sharif come? I haven't seen them for so long."

"It's difficult to travel, *Yaama*," Mama says in exasperation.

Sitti Zeynab ignores her. "Don't they miss their mother? How confident they are that I won't choke to death on a *kibbeh* tomorrow or get trampled on the dance floor at the wedding."

"Oh, *Yaama*," Mama says, walking up to Sitti Zeynab and giving her an affectionate squeeze of the shoulder. "Don't think bad thoughts."

"You know how excitable people get when the music comes on. I could be trampled, for who would notice a little old woman like me?"

"But you're not little!" Tariq blurts, sending us all, including Sitti Zeynab, into fits of laughter.

Later in the evening, Mama's friend Amto Samar visits with her three-year-old son, Hasan. Amto Samar, who isn't able to attend the wedding, wants to see Jihan's dress.

Jihan brings her dress into the living room and Amto Samar gushes and makes a fuss.

"*Masha Allah*, God be praised," Sitti Zeynab keeps muttering, glaring at Amto Samar. "You're going to jinx the dress with all this fuss! Praise God, will you? Is that crystal now loose and dangling off the bodice?"

"Oh, *Yaama*, would you relax?"

"I assure you I have the purest intentions and am not giving Jihan the evil eye," Amto Samar says tersely.

"The devil works in mysterious ways. I knew a woman once who had hair down to her waist. Her husband kept bragging about how silky it was. One day she woke up with half of it on the pillow and her legs hairer than my son-in-law's. How do you explain that?"

"Allergies?" Mama says, exchanging a conspiratorial look with Amto Samar.

"Pah!"

Then Baba walks in, turning the television on. "There's been a suicide bomb in Tel Aviv," he says grimly.

We sit down to watch the scenes of carnage on the screen. Ambulance sirens are wailing, blood is splashed on the street, people are running, screaming, and crying, their clothes soaked in blood.

I think of David and Mali and my heart races.

"Revenge achieves nothing," Baba mutters. He leans forward and puts his elbows on his thighs, hiding his head in his hands.

"It's madness," Sitti Zeynab says.

"We will all pay for this," Mama says with a sigh. "How can they think God will reward those who kill?"

Then suddenly megaphones blast outside and soldiers patrol the streets in armored personnel vehicles to declare that a curfew has been imposed. Amto Samar and Hasan are stuck with us.

Meanwhile, Hasan starts to scream his throat hoarse and we have no idea why.

"Mommy! It hurts!" he cries.

Baba paces the room helplessly. Mama and Amto Samar are hysterical.

"Maybe his appendix has burst!" Amto Samar cries.

"Maybe he has kidney stones."

"Mama!" Jihan yells. "He's *three*."

Hasan screams with pain and Amto Samar, helpless, sobs loudly.

"He could have been possessed by a jinn!" Sitti Zeynab offers. She starts to read verses from the Koran.

"What kind of jinn, Sitti?" Tariq asks. "Is it still here? Can I talk to it?"

"We need a doctor!" Baba cries.

Hasan continues to scream; Amto Samar wails; Sitti Zeynab prays; Mama blames Baba for not knowing what to do; Baba blames Mama for making things worse; and Jihan, Tariq, and I look on and argue over who will have to give up their space on the bed for Amto Samar and Hasan.

"I'm about to get married," Jihan says. "I need my beauty sleep. . . . Oh, wait . . . look at Hasan . . . he's touching . . ." She then storms over to Hasan, lifts him onto her lap, and holds him under the chin, tilting his face upward.

"Hey! He's got something in his nose!"

Amto Samar leaps over to Hasan and sweeps him into her arms.

"Wait," Baba says, "lay him down on the couch. Nur, get your eyebrow tweezers."

"A jinn could have put something in his nose," Sitti Zeynab says stubbornly, and continues to read her verses from the Koran.

Mama runs into the bedroom and returns, producing the tweezers. Hasan sees them and screams louder. Jihan, Amto Samar, and Mama hold Hasan down while Baba delicately removes the wheel of a toy car from Hasan's right nostril. We all cheer and Hasan, sniffling, buries his face in Amto Samar's chest.

"Who wants ice cream?" Mama cries, and Hasan nods enthusiastically.

It's our last container of peppermint chocolate swirl. Mama always insists on reserving desserts in the freezer for possible guests. It's madness because nobody is allowed to go visiting during curfews anyway. So we always fight with her to let us eat the desserts during curfew time. She rarely acquiesces.

Tonight, Mama stops being stubborn and allows Hasan, Tariq, and me to eat a first *and* second helping of the peppermint chocolate swirl. We even lick the lid and container until not a drop is left. We refuse to let Baba taste it because he's an accomplice with Mama whenever we want ice cream at other times. The three of us sleep on the living room floor (Amto Samar and Hasan get the bed), smelling of sugar.

We refuse to brush our teeth, so the aftertaste will last a little longer. I wake up in the middle of the night to hear Sitti Zeynab bent over Hasan. She's praying to God not to allow a jinn to stick a toy up his left nostril. With the prospect of ice cream as a reward for his troubles, I pray that a jinn will.

TWENTY-THREE

Baba makes the necessary calls the night before Jihan's wedding. We sit around him, listening to him repeat his friends' travel reports.

"What? A complete restriction for all Palestinian vehicles along road 465? Where is that? North of Ramallah? Will it affect us?"

"Ask him if it will affect us!" Mama says.

"I just did!" Baba snaps. "What? He says — wait, Hany, let me tell Nur — he says the villages of Husan, Battir, and al-Walaja can only leave their area on foot."

"But they're west of here," Mama says. "We should be fine, yes?"

"Yes. He also says there are flying checkpoints — excuse me? Oh, that's in the Hebron district."

"OK, well, that has nothing to do with us! Oof!"

"Yes, I know. No, I'm talking to Nur. Well, do you think the Container will be OK? You don't know. *Ya zalami*, I know you can't be sure. . . ."

We wake up at dawn the next morning. Baba drives Jihan and me to the hairdresser where a crotchety man with a jet-black toupee straightens our hair into submission. A cigarette dangles from his lips as if by an invisible thread. I can't keep my eyes away from the ash that grows as the cigarette burns. He pulls and tugs at my hair till the roots feel as though they're on fire. His brow furrows, his eyes squint in concentration. Beads of perspiration hover just below his fake hairline. But the ash never drops. In the final second he somehow knows when to butt it in the pineapple-shaped ashtray. When at last the hair has been singed and the natural curls banished, the curling tongs are produced. *Click, clack,* his hands deftly maneuver the piping-hot tongs, like a magician balancing sticks of fire. My hair is again pulled and tugged until at last it's all curled, half of it swept back high on my head with a pink ribbon for full effect.

When Jihan's hair has been piled high and hair-sprayed into obedience, she conducts a thorough inspection of my hair. "Perfect," she declares and then leads me out to the car where Baba is waiting.

The makeup artist, Shams, arrives at our apartment almost as soon as we return. She packs so much makeup on Jihan's face that I wonder if Jihan will need a chisel to remove it. Shams then fusses over Mama while I help Sitti Zeynab change into a loose, light-colored *galabiya*. Her hands tremble as I help her put her rings on. When I'm finished, I kiss her right hand, raise it to my forehead, and then kiss it again.

Mama emerges from the living room half an hour later, her eyes brightened with kohl, her cheeks contoured and rosy, her lips smooth and red. Pride swells within me. She catches my glance and smiles shyly.

"Where is your sister?" she asks.

"Waiting for you to help her put her dress on."

She goes into the bedroom and Shams steps out of the living room and calls my name.

The muscles in my neck tense as I see her eyes follow my scars.

"Hmm, we'll have to use extra foundation," she says, tapping her hand on her chin as she studies her makeup box. "Don't worry. I can hide your scars the way I hide my acne. You're gorgeous anyway. Look at your big eyes. And those cheekbones. Just like your mother. Not even the bride has that sort of definition, but that's between you and me, yes?"

She grins at me and I try not to laugh. She orders me to sit down and wipes my face clean with a baby wipe. She hums and talks to herself as she works on my face. "Hmm, not that color, too light . . . Ahh, yes, that's perfect. . . ."

When at last she's finished, I wait with trepidation as she retrieves a hand mirror from her box. I almost burst into tears of relief when I see that she's covered my scars under layers of foundation and powder. I sit still, mirror in my hand, studying my face. For the first time since that day, I feel beautiful again.

When we're all ready, we wait for Jihan and Mama in the living room. Mohammed is dressed in a baby tuxedo and sits in my lap, gargling and cooing over his red bow tie. Tariq and I take turns devouring him with kisses. Baba and Sitti Zeynab keep staring at me, commenting on how beautiful I look, making me blush.

"A beauty!" Sitti Zeynab gushes. "The beauty of the family!"

"What about Jihan?" Tariq asks.

"Yes, yes, she's beautiful, as every bride should be, but look at Hayaat. Just look at her! *Amar*, the moon! Luminous!"

Tariq thinks for a moment. "I'm telling Jihan," he says.

"Come here," Baba says. Tariq is only too happy to jump onto Baba's lap.

At last the bedroom door opens and Mama emerges. "Oh, she's breathtaking," she cries, fanning her face with her hand. "Thank God this is waterproof. Oh, Foad, just you wait and see your eldest daughter. Just you wait and see."

And then Jihan steps into the living room. Sitti Zeynab starts ululating and Jihan beams at us. Her eyes catch Baba's. He reaches his arms out to her and it's the first time I've ever seen him cry.

Baba receives the telephone call advising that the groom is on his way. We hear the incessant bleating of car horns in the distance, the beeping becoming louder when the cars and service vans enter our street. Tariq and I rush to the window and see boys and a group of men surrounding Ahmad, performing *al-zaffeh*, the traditional wedding song. A man pounds down on a large drum strung around his waist. His eyes are ablaze in his ruddy face, and some of the men and women form a circle and dance the *dabka* around him, beating the ground with their feet as though they wish to alert the earth that it, too, should rejoice in Ahmad and Jihan's union. The party claps and sings around Ahmad, chanting:

> *Our bridegroom is the best of youth, the best of youth is our bridegroom.*
> *Our bridegroom is Antar Abs, Antar Abs is our bridegroom.*
> *The sun which is in the sky, knows that we have a bridegroom on our earth today.*
> *Our bridegroom is the sun of the dawn, he asked the bride's hand and wasn't shy.*

We help Jihan negotiate her dress down the flights of stairs. I notice Jihan's hands are shaking. Baba squeezes one of them tightly and gives her a tender smile.

When we reach the first floor, Ahmad steps into the doorway. He kisses and hugs Baba and Mama. I take in his goofy smile as he looks at Jihan, and I marvel at how fragile his love for Jihan has made him. Happiness swells within me.

"But where are your parents?" Baba asks.

"Mama was so excited, she forgot her card and she couldn't get through the checkpoint," Ahmad replies.

"Oh, what a shame," Baba says.

Mama laughs. "I don't blame her. I nearly forgot my purse, I've been so anxious!"

"They're waiting for us in Ramallah," Ahmad says.

My immediate thought is that all the cleaning Mama made us do was for nothing. There will be no in-laws to admire the scent of disinfectant in the house and the sparkling kitchen cabinets.

Jihan takes her seat beside Ahmad in the backseat of the wedding car. White ribbons and streamers that are attached to the trunk flap in the gentle breeze. We climb into a service minivan. Mama sits beside Tariq, Mohammed on her lap. Sitti Zeynab sits beside me, and Baba sits alone. Samy, Amto Christina, and Amo Joseph, along with some of the other Bethlehem guests, fill the remaining seats. The driver of the wedding car, Ahmad's best friend, beeps the horn and pulls out from the curb. We follow closely behind. Other guests have hired a couple of service minivans and are tailing us, followed by the party of people who have accompanied Ahmad. The drivers honk and beep through the streets and people look at us and wave.

Abu Mazen has brought along a small *daraboka* and begins to play. We sing and cheer. I look at Samy and he grins at me.

We drive along Wadi al-Nar. When we reach the Container checkpoint, my stomach twists into knots. The line of cars and taxis is impossibly long. It's sensible that we've left before noon given that the wedding starts at five. Ramallah is only about thirteen miles away but it may as well be one hundred.

The soldiers examine identity cards. Jihan turns back to face us through the rear window. There's a weary expression on her face and she leans her head on Ahmad's shoulder.

Thirty-five long minutes pass. Mohammed cries for every single one of them. He refuses to go to Baba or me. Sitti Zeynab, trying to make him smile, flashes him a toothless grin and he screams the roof down. Tariq jumps up from his seat and hops on one foot, making the monkey sounds that usually send Mohammed into an uncontrollable fit of giggles. But Mohammed is in no mood. The other passengers bleat out useless comments. "Check his diaper." "Maybe he's hungry." "An earache?"

Mama is fed up. She hands Mohammed to me and storms out of the minivan, ignoring Baba's shouts for her to calm down as he follows after her.

"How much longer?" she demands of a soldier. "My son is crying! It's our daughter's wedding! We want to pass!"

"You must wait," he says and slowly walks to the wedding car. He motions for the driver, Jihan, and Ahmad to exit the car.

"But her dress will get dirty!" Mama cries.

"Go back," he says crossly. "This won't take long."

"It's enough!" Mama suddenly screams hysterically. "Do we look like terrorists to you?"

"It's OK, it's OK," Baba nervously reassures the soldier. "She's going back. No trouble."

"Mama!" I yell out from the window, over Mohammed's cries. "Please come back!"

Baba quickly takes Mama's arm and leads her back to the service. Satisfied, the soldier turns back to the car. Mama sinks into her seat and stares moodily out of the window. Mohammed continues to cry and I rock him in my arms, not daring to burden Mama with him.

"*Ya* Nur, wipe your tears," Amto Christina says. "We'll pass eventually."

Ahmad steps out of the car first. Jihan tries to get out, but her dress is so big that she has to first lift up the layers at the front to avoid stepping on the satin. Ahmad leans down to help her and she eventually manages to get out without tripping on the dress.

"Her dress. The dirt . . ." one of the guests says with a cluck of her tongue.

"That's why white dresses make no sense," Samy says to me.

Ahmad places a protective hand on Jihan's arm. The soldier says something to Ahmad, and Ahmad reaches into his pocket and produces his identity card. Jihan opens her small white clutch and retrieves her card too. The soldier glances at the cards and then nods, flicking his hand to indicate his permission for them to reboard the car.

Sitti Zeynab turns to Abu Mazen and orders him to play. "God knows we'll send Jihan off with laughter and dance," she says and starts to clap her hands. We all start to sing.

"*Yallah*, stop crying and join in, Nur," Sitti Zeynab scolds. "Things could be worse."

"Yes, *Yaama*," Mama says automatically.

When Ahmad and Jihan have settled back in the car, Jihan turns to face us from the rear window and waves energetically.

"Hooray!" we cry and continue singing and tapping our hands against the back of the seats to the beat of the *daraboka*.

Qalandiya terminal is next to come. Our service joins the line of cars, vans, and taxis waiting to pass through the vehicle crossing. We disembark. Mama rushes over to the wedding car and helps Jihan out. Mama, Amto Christina, and I try to lift Jihan's wedding dress off the ground as we lead her through to the passenger crossing.

We enter the terminal. It's a maze of revolving metal doors, metal detectors, and metal passageways. It reminds me of a farm pen I saw on a show on television once. The line is long and people stare at Jihan and Ahmad and offer their congratulations. When it's Jihan's turn, we help her negotiate her dress through the turnstiles. Mama is frustrated and is swearing out loud. Ahmad is grim but calm. Jihan is obviously annoyed but manages to joke about the situation.

"Are you going to come to my rescue when they pass the metal detectors under my hoop?" she teases Ahmad.

"I'll break their legs if they dare," Ahmad says, but we all know his bravado is meaningless. We laugh for his sake anyway.

When Jihan squeezes through a turnstile and the buzzer sounds loudly, a soldier approaches her and quickly passes a metal detector over her body.

"It's my jewelry," Jihan explains.

"I'm sorry, I have to check," the soldier says. He is

young, probably nineteen, with a smooth face and big gray eyes.

Jihan looks back and calls out to us: "At least I know my husband is generous. Look how much I'm buzzing."

"She has a point," Baba says to Ahmad. "She has enough gold on her to hold us all up until tomorrow."

An hour later we've all passed through the checks to meet our service vans on the other side. We help Jihan back into the car, and Mama hands her a bag filled with deodorant, scented baby wipes, and perfume.

"Here, freshen up," she insists.

We enter Ramallah soon after, singing loudly, blaring our arrival to the streets. It's a Friday, the most popular day for weddings, and we're not the only wedding party on the roads competing for the attention of onlookers.

We arrive at the reception. Ahmad's parents are waiting, and the small crowd outside the hall claps and cheers. Guests go inside and take their seats. We all kiss and hug Ahmad's parents and family. Ahmad's mother plants a lipstick mark on Mama's cheek. One of Ahmad's aunts has breath that stinks of garlic.

The hall owner is waiting to lead us to the bridal-party room.

"See you inside," I say to Samy, and he follows after Amto Christina and Amo Joseph.

Amto Somaia, who's met us at the front, takes Sitti Zeynab inside to sit her down. I follow Mama, Baba, and Tariq to the bridal-party room, Mohammed in my arms.

"I'm so nervous!" Jihan says.

Mama is wiping the lipstick mark off her face. "You'll be fine!"

"Baba, remember to wave to the guests when you enter," Jihan says.

"Yes, yes, of course."

"And make sure the cameraman gets a shot of you smiling to him and waving."

"Yes, *habibti*." Baba turns to Ahmad's father. "Like an army general, eh?" They both laugh.

Jihan focuses on Tariq next. "Tariq, you better not mess up! Remember how we practiced? You walk in with Suzanne, Hayaat, and Mohammed, and someone from the hall will show you all where to stand."

"Who's Suzanne?"

"Ahmad's cousin. You know that."

"Mohammed can't walk."

Jihan rolls her eyes. "Hayaat is holding him, silly."

"Well, I don't want to hold her hand!"

"We've already discussed this," Jihan says through gritted teeth.

"Well, I won't. She's a girl."

"*Tariq.*"

"She won't bite," Ahmad says, giving Suzanne an affectionate hug. Suzanne looks at Tariq and hisses.

Tariq pokes his tongue out at her and Jihan flashes him a menacing look. "I'll clobber you if you mess up!"

The hall owner enters. "It's time," he says.

We line up outside the double doors, our nervous chatter suddenly drowned out by loud music and the sound of the MC announcing Ahmad's parents. The doors open and Ahmad's parents walk into the hall. The hall erupts into clapping.

Mama and Baba are next. "I'm so nervous!" Mama exclaims, burying her head against Baba's shoulder. He kisses the top of her head. Their affection startles me. I feel warm and tingly inside.

"I'll still look like the silliest person in the bridal party," he says, "so you have nothing to worry about."

When the MC calls our names we step through the large double door onto a long red carpet. The hall is enormous. More than three hundred guests watch us walk up the carpet to join the bridal party. Mohammed, overwhelmed, is quiet in my arms, too busy looking at everybody. Tariq and Suzanne are barely touching each other's hands but are at least standing beside each other. Everybody is watching us, looking at our faces, clapping, and smiling. Sitti Zeynab is at the head table and we exchange grins. I'm nervous and shy but exhilarated by the buzz in the air and the joyfulness of the music.

We take our place next to Mama and Baba and the MC invites everybody to stand up in preparation for Ahmad and Jihan's entrance. The doors open and the couple enter slowly, the *zaffeh* party leading their way. Two men pound large drums strung to their waists. Another man plays the *oud*. Two others jump and dance in front of Ahmad and Jihan, leading them to the dance floor in the middle of the hall. The guests clap and cheer and leave their seats to join the *zaffeh*. I join a *dabka* line and we make our way in a circle around Ahmad and Jihan, who are dancing in the center.

Samy runs up to me and cuts into the *dabka* line, taking my hand and relieving me from the sweaty palm of the oversized woman beside me. He leans close to my ear. Yelling at the top of his voice to ensure I hear over the deafeningly loud music, he says: "Ahmad's father tripped when he came in!"

I let out a hoot of laughter. "No!"

"It was hilarious. His foot caught on the carpet and he stumbled forward. He was fine, though. But his face was bright red!"

The crowd suddenly lifts Ahmad onto their shoulders and then raises Jihan on a chair. I gasp, praying she won't fall.

"The chair has a satin sheet on it!" I tell Samy.

"So?"

"So her dress will slip! She'll fall! She looks terrified."

"No, she doesn't. She's laughing. Ahmad looks more worried. Those two guys holding him up don't look as though they have enough meat on them to hold up Mohammed."

But they don't fall. The lights of the chandeliers shine on Jihan's warm, animated face as Ahmad holds her hands in the air and the crowd chants and claps.

The rest of the night passes like a comet. Samy and I dance every *dabka*. We hang out with my cousins from Ramallah. Nawal is also thirteen and Hakim is fourteen. When we tire of dancing, we grab our desserts and sit on the edge of the hall, away from the crowds of people still feverishly dancing around Ahmad and Jihan.

"So yeah, we snuck into Jerusalem," Samy boasts, taking a big bite of his cake.

"No way!"

"You didn't!"

Samy nods and gives Nawal and Hakim a casual shrug. "It was easy. Jumped the Wall and we were in. We had Israelis with us. Hayaat instantly liked them but I wasn't fooled for a minute. Just ignore Hayaat rolling her eyes there. At least one of us had to be shrewd. I had to break them down first. Assess whether they were from *Mossad* or the *Shabak*. I know these things, on account of my father. I can detect an agent a mile away. They were OK in the end."

"Wow," Nawal coos, and I want to gag.

"So tell us more," Hakim says in awe.

Samy picks a tooth and then tilts his head to the side. "Well, we managed to get to the Old City, but there was a huge protest. There were tanks and planes and a missile or two."

"*Samy!*"

"Hayaat, you passed out, remember? You weren't in the thick of the action. I never explained the situation fully to you."

"No, but Yossi did and he never mentioned planes or missiles."

Samy gives me a dismissive wave. "He didn't want to agitate you any further." He turns to Nawal and Hakim. "After Hayaat lost me —"

"Excuse me, *you* lost me."

"Let him finish," Nawal says.

"Yeah, Hayaat, we want to hear," Hakim adds.

I scowl at them and fold my arms over my chest. "Fine, go on. I'm always up for some storytelling."

Nawal and Hakim flash Samy smiles of support. Samy, puffing his chest out, shoots me a triumphant look.

"A soldier grabbed me! Threw a sack over my head and dragged me to a jeep."

"What did they do to you?"

"Did they torture you? We know a guy, Sofyan, who got busted in Jerusalem for traveling without the permit. They beat him up badly. What did they do to you?"

"Tell us, Samy!"

"I managed to escape. I took advantage of the chaos and slipped away. The soldier must have been new on the job. He didn't tie my hands and feet up. But he did threaten to attach electrodes to my chest and set dogs on me. When he threw me in the back of the jeep and went away to round more people up, I took the sack off my head and snuck out. The air was filled with smoke and the planes were really loud so I was able to escape back onto the streets to rescue Hayaat."

"*Rescue me?* What about Yossi?" I shake my head in disbelief but he ignores me.

"Wow! You're so brave," Nawal gushes.

"That's amazing!" Hakim declares.

"Some questions," I say. "Did the soldier leave you without anyone to guard you? Did he just leave the jeep open? Are you telling me he wanted to give you some fresh air? And why is this the first time I'm hearing about —"

"Oh look, they're starting the speeches," Samy says, standing up. "We better go. My aunt will have a fit if I'm not at the table. She's really into manners, you know how it is."

"Yeah, we do," Hakim says with a sigh, and Nawal nods enthusiastically.

"Come find us when they've finished," Nawal says. "I want to hear all about how you rescued Hayaat!"

I storm off and Samy follows me, collapsing with laughter.

"I don't see the joke," I say.

"Oh, come on, it was fun! Did you see their faces?"

"Rescuing me? What are you going to say? You arrived in the Batmobile?"

He claps his hands. "They'd probably fall for it! Anyway, the wedding was getting boring. I had to spice it up."

I grunt and he laughs again.

"Come on, let's see how far we can take it."

"Well, if you get to escape from the jeep I get to drive Yossi's car between two tanks."

He gives me an incredulous look. "That's brilliant. Why didn't I think of that?"

After the speeches, Samy and I combine our efforts and sufficently traumatize and impress my cousins. When we've had enough, I take a seat next to Sitti Zeynab, leaning my head against her shoulder.

We stare out at Jihan and Ahmad, who are being kissed good-bye by a long line of guests.

"I'll miss her, the rascal," Sitti Zeynab says to me and dabs her eyes. "But she looks so happy. God grant them happiness and many babies. God protect them and their families and Um Ahmad . . ."

For once I let her continue without interruption.

The evening eventually approaches its end. We have to leave earlier than usual to ensure we pass the check-points before they close.

"*Yallah, yallah,*" Baba says anxiously. "We can't risk being stuck in Ramallah. We must return before they close the gate."

We hold on to Jihan under an inky sky and an array of brilliant stars, tears of joy and sorrow streaming down our faces.

"Live in Bethlehem," Mama wails, clinging on to Jihan. "Please, Ahmad, don't take her from us."

"It's OK, Mama," Jihan says through tears. "We'll . . . visit . . . I . . . promise."

"You must! You must!" Mama bursts into a fresh wave of tears and Baba self-consciously steps toward Mama, wrapping his arm around her.

"Come back with us!" Tariq screams, clutching on to Jihan's dress. Exhausted at being awake far past his bedtime, he starts to howl, prompting Baba to pick him up. Tariq rests his head on Baba's shoulder and sobs.

"I'll look after her," Ahmad says, "I promise you all."

"We know you will," Baba says.

"I'll break you if I hear otherwise," Sitti Zeynab says and we laugh.

"Consult me for recipes!" Mama reminds Jihan. "And call me every day. Any time is fine, but it's better to call after dinner so I can speak to you without interruption. And, Ahmad, I promise I'll send you my pickled cucumbers. I know how much you are deprived of good ones. And —"

Jihan takes a step toward me, leaving Ahmad to deal with Mama. She takes my hands and pulls me close to her. I hug her tightly and she kisses me.

"You must visit," she says. "I know it's hard but please try."

"Of course we will."

"And call me. As much as you like. Keep me up to date with all the Bethlehem gossip."

"Jihan," Ahmad says gently, touching her arm. "The car is waiting."

"And we must start moving," Baba insists.

Jihan envelops me in a massive hug and I struggle not to cry. Then she pulls back and smiles at us all. "How exciting!" she cries. "I'm married!"

Sitti Zeynab starts ululating and Mama laughs as she wipes the tears from her face. The wind whispers in the pine and olive trees, telling us to let her go.

And eventually we do.

In the long drive on our way back, I rest my head against Baba's shoulder, stare out into a star-filled night, and think about the last few weeks.

I am thirteen years old and I know what blood is. I know what loss is. I know the smell of a corpse. I know the shape of a body flattened under a tank. I know the dusty clouds left behind a frenzied bulldozer. The Wall will soon be finished. Parts of Bethlehem will be fully deserted: businesses closed, houses abandoned, streets emptied, schools sliced in half. I'm living in an open-air prison.

But I won't live in despair. Because I'm thirteen years old and this is what I also know:

That so long as there is life there'll be love. That I'll learn to love the mirror as surely as I have learned to think of Maysaa and smile. That the past can both torment and heal. That I'll do more than survive. That in the end we are all of us only human beings who laugh the same, and that one day the world will realize that we simply want to live as a free people, with hope and dignity and purpose. That is all.

GLOSSARY OF
ARABIC WORDS

abaya: a loose robe covering the body

abeet: stupid

abu: father of; honorific term that incorporates the father's firstborn son's name into the father's own, e.g., if the father's firstborn son is "Yusuf," the father takes the name "Abu Yusuf"

Adra: the Virgin, i.e., the Virgin Mary

ahlan: hello

al-Fatiha: opening chapter of the Koran

Alhamdulilah: Praise be to Allah

Allah yerda alaikum: God be pleased with you

al-Quds: Jerusalem

al-zaffeh: the traditional wedding song

amar: moon

ameen: amen

amo: paternal uncle; also used by children to address adult males as a sign of respect

amto: paternal aunt; also used by children to address adult females as a sign of respect

argeela: water pipe

assalamu alaikom: peace be upon you (an Arabic greeting)

dabka: a traditional Arabic folk dance

daraboka: drumlike musical instrument from the Middle East

deir: village

dua: prayer or supplication

dunam: a unit of land that is equal to about a quarter of an acre

Eid: Muslim religious festival

galabiya: long traditional gown worn in the Middle East

ghada: main meal/dinner

habibi: my darling (to a male)

habibti: my darling (to a female)

Haji: Islamic honorific title

hawiya: Palestinian identification card

hijab: a veil with which a Muslim woman covers her hair

homaar: donkey

inshallah: God willing

itfadalo: welcome

katb al-kitaab: Islamic marriage contract

keffiyeh: headdress worn by Arab men

khalo: maternal uncle

khalto: maternal aunt

kibbeh: a dish of ground lamb and bulgur

knafa: traditional Arabic dessert

labne: thickened yogurt

la ilaha ilalah: there is only one God

majaneen: crazy people

majnoon: crazy

maklobe: traditional Arabic dish made from rice, chicken or meat, and fried eggplant

mansaf: traditional Palestinian dish made from lamb cooked in a yogurt sauce and served with rice

Masha Allah: God be praised

momtaz: excellent

naseeb: fate

nur ayni: light of my eyes

oghti: sister

ostaz: sir

ostaza: miss

oud: Middle Eastern lute

Rab: God

raka'a: the bowing position in the Muslim prayer

salam: a greeting meaning "peace"

salamtik: your health/safety

shabab: young men

sidi: my grandfather

sido: grandfather

sito: grandmother

sitti: my grandmother

souk: market

um: mother of; honorific term that incorporates the mother's firstborn son's name into the mother's own, e.g., if the mother's firstborn son is "Yusuf," the mother takes the name "Um Yusuf"

Wallah: I swear by God

ya: oh

yaama: oh mother (respectful form of addressing one's own mother, often used in villages)